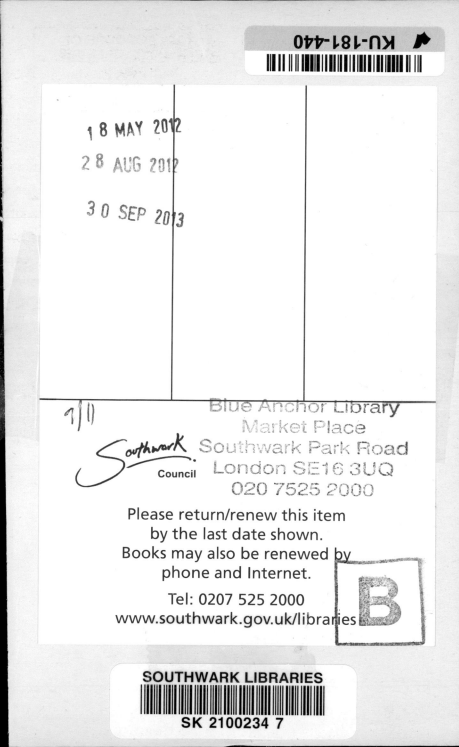

Cora Harrison is the author of many successful books for children and adults. She lives on a small farm in the west of Ireland with her husband, her German Shepherd dog called Oscar and a very small white cat called Polly.

Find out more about Cora at:
www.coraharrison.com

To discover why Cora wrote
the London Murder Mysteries, head online to:
www.piccadillypress.co.uk/londonmurdermysteries

The London Murder Mysteries

The Montgomery Murder
The Deadly Fire
Murder on Stage
Death of a Chimney Sweep
The Body in the Fog *(coming soon)*
Death In Devil's Acre *(coming soon)*

THE LONDON MURDER MYSTERIES

DEATH OF A CHIMNEY SWEEP

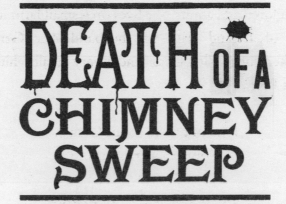

CORA HARRISON

PICCADILLY PRESS • LONDON

First published in Great Britain in 2011
by Piccadilly Press Ltd,
5 Castle Road, London NW1 8PR
www.piccadillypress.co.uk

A catalogue record for this book is available
from the British Library

ISBN: 978 1 84812 159 1 (paperback)

1 3 5 7 9 10 8 6 4 2

Printed in the UK by CPI Bookmarque, Croydon, CR0 4TD
Cover design by Patrick Knowles
Cover illustration by Chris King

For my grandson,
Shane Mason

CHAPTER 1

WHY DID HE DIE?

Alfie knew who it was the moment he saw the body. It lay there on the river steps, just by Hungerford Bridge. Soot-blackened clothes, soot-blackened hair, soot-blackened skin, dead eyes staring at nothing. If it hadn't been for a sudden beam of light from a fishing boat, he would never have noticed it lying against the darkness of the rain-washed stone. But he did see it, and then he could not walk away.

Early that morning, Alfie had been coming down St Martin's Lane when he saw the figure of Joe, the young chimney sweep, silhouetted against the dawn sky, scrambling hastily across the rooftops.

Joe had been in a state when he reached the ground. His words were almost incomprehensible. Something about a bend . . . something about going the wrong way – or was it going into the wrong room? . . . something about being scared . . .

Alfie had tried to persuade him to run away, but Joe did not want to take that drastic step. Runaway apprentices were put in prison.

So the boy had gone back to the chimneys, back to Grimston the master chimney sweep. And now he was dead.

But how did he die?

Alfie looked all around. The light was fading on this winter afternoon and the fog was coming down thickly again. The river and the shoreline below were already dark as night.

The oil lamps from Hungerford market were a golden haze in the distance, and a few pitch torches on the roadway flared in small pockets of light, but there was no sign of anyone nearby.

Had the terrified boy just lain down and died?

Or had Joe been murdered?

CHAPTER 2

DANGER

'What's the matter?' Sammy, Alfie's blind brother, had stayed silent up to now. Sammy always knew when something was wrong; when fear, anger – even terror – overwhelmed his older brother.

'A dead body. Joe the sweeping boy,' said Alfie briefly.

'Dead!' echoed Sammy. 'What happened?'

'Don't know.' And then, after a minute, almost to himself, Alfie said, 'Why here? Why by Hungerford Bridge? Grimston has all his boys up in that stable at the back of Westminster Abbey. Why should Joe come down here?'

'Bit early to have stopped work, too,' observed Sammy. 'The four o'clock bell at St Martin's church has only just gone.'

Alfie bent down over the body, trying hard to see it properly, but it was only a shadowy outline. At that moment, an anchored ship swung with the turning tide and its lamps lit up the scene. The light splashed over the body, showing the blackened young face – no sign of a wound, but a tongue protruded.

Alfie drew in a deep breath. 'He was murdered, Sammy,' he whispered in his brother's ear. 'Someone strangled him!'

'Alfie,' said Sammy in a low voice, 'that gig that passed in front of us a minute ago, just as we was coming out of the alleyway – I'd say that they was the ones that dumped the body. I heard a thud and then they pulled the horse's head around and went back towards the market.'

Alfie knelt down and touched the body. It was still warm. He lifted the arm; it was limp.

Alfie knew death well. After every night of frost or fog or even rain, there would be bodies on the London streets – some under the carts at Hungerford market, some in shop doorways, some under the archways of Waterloo Bridge. Joe would be just another body to be carted away when morning came.

'Alfie,' said Sammy, his voice full of alarm, 'that gig is coming back . . .'

Thoughts darted through Alfie's mind like lightning. They were in danger if it was the same man, the man who threw the dead body out of the gig. The sudden light on the river bank would have made him look back and he would have seen the two boys by the body. He might think he'd been spotted by Sammy and Alfie – in that case, he'd want to get rid of them. One dead boy, three dead boys; one murder, three murders – what was the difference in the mind of a killer?

It was no good running. Hungerford market, crowded with stalls and people, was a good hundred yards away; a horse with only a light, open-topped carriage attached could outrun any boy.

A second later, Alfie was in the evil-smelling water of the Thames. He held Sammy in a tight grip around the blind boy's chest, pulling him along, making for a place to hide. The outline of the boat was now just a dark shadow against the brick pillar of the bridge. There was no one on it. If they could get there without being seen, it would be a safe hiding place for them.

The water was getting deeper – up to their waists now. Alfie prayed that it would go no higher. He tried to move as silently as possible, pushing his legs forward in long smooth strides, and Sammy copied him.

'Hi! Is there someone there?' The shout made him jump. The oil lantern had been lifted off the gig and its beam swung along the shoreline. Alfie stopped for a moment and then moved cautiously forward for a few more yards. In front of them were the steps leading up to the bridge and the boat was moored beside them. He reached out and touched the solid brick of the pier. Cautiously, Alfie turned Sammy around until the boy had his back to the steps and pressed on his shoulders. His breath grew short and his heart thudded as he tried to make Sammy understand what he wanted him to do. He did not dare whisper and had to guide the blind boy by touch. Every moment he expected the light of the lantern to reveal them to the man hunting them. Finally his groping hand found wood and he gripped the side of the boat tightly.

'Stay still,' he whispered in Sammy's ear.

Once he was over the edge of the boat and his feet were firmly on the deck, he helped Sammy in. By touch he found a tarpaulin and pushed Sammy under it. He was just about to tuck his own head under it when the lamp's beam swung in a wide arc and lit up the fishing boat.

Had they been seen?

CHAPTER 3

HIDING PLACE

For a moment the light stayed focused on the boat, lighting up the canvas covering them, but then it moved on and Alfie drew in a sigh of relief. The stench of fish was almost overpowering, but the solid roof of tarpaulin over their heads gave a sense of security. Alfie strained his ears but could hear no sound. No one shouted; no footsteps approached from the bridge. Perhaps they had not been seen. Perhaps his luck had held. Sammy moved cautiously and Alfie stiffened, but then heard a muted chuckle.

'There's an eel here, a dead eel, just under my hand,' whispered Sammy and Alfie smiled into the darkness. Although Sammy was only eleven, he was amazingly brave. He had been blind since he was a small child – blind from the spotted fever, but it was years since Alfie heard him complain. The boys' grandfather had always impressed on Sammy that he was cleverer and more talented than anyone else around and perhaps that had given him a belief in himself, a serene courage and a keen sense of humour.

'Supper,' Alfie whispered back, but could not stop himself from adding, 'if we get out of here alive.'

However, as the minutes passed, his confidence grew. Surely, if the man came onto the bridge and shone his lantern in their direction, then they'd see its glow. But no light came. Everything was as black as midnight and the splash of the water against the bridge was the only sound to be heard.

The only sound to be heard by Alfie, at least.

Sammy sat up suddenly, his head lifting up the tarpaulin.

Alfie waited, holding his breath, not daring even to whisper.

'It's going away,' said Sammy after a minute. 'The gig is moving. I hear the horse. Listen, you can hear, one wheel is a little loose. Hear it rumble.'

Alfie listened. He could hear nothing, but he

trusted Sammy. He was not a boy to speak without being sure.

'Gone now,' said Sammy, but he still spoke in a low voice. 'It's turned up towards Charing Cross.'

Alfie sat up and moved his legs. He was soaked through and freezing. Now that the tension was over, his teeth began to chatter.

'Let's get out of here before we freeze to death,' he said, but Sammy's hand fumbled to cover Alfie's mouth.

'Shh,' he said and then added in Alfie's ear, 'Someone on the bridge.'

Alfie could hear this now. A loud, confident tread, someone wearing heavy hobnailed boots. Could it be the boatman?

Come back for his eel, he thought. Despite his terror, he found himself desperately trying to suppress a giggle.

The footsteps stopped on the bridge just above the boat. Their owner seemed to pause there, not coming down the steps towards the boat. And then there was a strong smell, a smell of tar, pungent enough to overcome the stench of dead fish. Alfie sighed with relief. Ten huge pitch torches were stuck into holders along both sides of the bridge. The one above their heads had just been lit. It would make getting out of the boat easier, but it also meant that they would be seen more easily. They would have to be very careful.

Alfie waited for what seemed like an eternity and then he peered out from under the tarpaulin. The bridge was lit up now and several big boats on the Thames had lanterns hanging from their masts. The lights were bright at Hungerford market and he knew that once he and Sammy got there, it would be easy to mingle with the crowds. The man in the gig could not have seen much of them down there by the water's edge – just a glimpse of two boys, one bending over the body thrown on the ground.

However, there was no one on the bridge and that's where they would have to be careful. Their two figures would be very noticeable. He thought about wading through the water again, but could not face it. Already he was shaking with the cold and he could hear Sammy's teeth chatter.

Getting Sammy out of the boat was agonisingly slow. Usually Alfie directed his brother with words, but now he dared not speak, and kept casting hunted glances over each shoulder as he steadied Sammy, lifting one bare foot after the other and making sure that the boy was safely on the stone steps before leading upwards. Through it all, Sammy kept a tight hold on the eel and this added to the difficulties.

Once they were up the steps and on the bridge, Alfie began to breathe more easily. The pitch torches flamed, but they cast black shadows and it was easy to creep from shadow to shadow until they reached the end of the bridge and were in the open space in front of the rotting old houses by the waterside. Alfie dragged Sammy quickly past these. Many of the men standing around specialized in fishing out dead bodies from the river – emptying the pockets of the corpses before handing them over to the police for a small reward. It was rumoured that a few of them were not above killing someone, dumping the body in the river, then fishing it out a few hours later – just so that the reward could be claimed!

No rewards for finding a corpse on the street, thought Alfie as they climbed the short steep hill to Charing Cross. The river, however, was a different matter. A few dead bodies there and cholera would begin to spread through the city of London. It was worthwhile to pay the riverside characters to trawl through the filthy water to remove drowned men and women before they began to decay.

'I'm freezing,' he said to Sammy as they passed

through Hungerford market.

'Think of the eel!' said Sammy through chattering teeth. 'Think of this big, fat, juicy eel roasting above a lovely hot fire.' He chuckled and swung the creature at his side.

Alfie laughed. 'We'll heat some beer and toast some bread and put chunks of fried eel on top of it,' he said to Sammy and a woman in a nearby stall gave him a sympathetic grin, her eyes on the eel swinging from Sammy's hand. They were all poor too; they knew the pleasure of an unexpected meal.

It felt good to be in the middle of a crowd and it felt good to be able to talk aloud. It would have been much quicker to get to Bow Street by going along the river, but Alfie shuddered with fear as well as with cold when he thought of the man in the gig driving his horse up and down, looking for him and his brother.

He tried not to think of anything other than the toasted eel, but one thought would keep coming into his head. What was he going to do about the murdered body of Joe the chimney sweep?

CHAPTER 4

ALFIE MAKES UP
HIS MIND

Alfie and Sammy, along with their two cousins, Jack and Tom, had lived in a small, damp cellar on Bow Street since the death of their mother over two years before. There were times when they all went hungry and there were times when Alfie worried about where the rent would come from at the end of each week – but, on the whole, they managed.

There was one thing that they usually had and that was warmth. Twelve-year-old Jack scavenged most days for coal along the shoreline and in the water of the river Thames, picking it up piece by piece, until he had enough to fill a sack. And then he wheeled the sack back to the cellar and sometimes started again, or sometimes helped one of the other boys with their street performances.

Sammy was the main earner of the gang. He had a glorious voice as well as a quick brain, and such a good memory that, if he heard a song once or twice, he could sing it back perfectly. People passing in the streets could not resist stopping and listening to him sing, and pennies or even sixpences soon tumbled into the bowl at his feet.

When Alfie and Sammy arrived home, still dripping with river water, the cellar was already lit up by a great fire. With a quick bark, Mutsy bounded across the floor, shaking the heavy fringe of hair from his eyes. Alfie could hardly see him in the darkness by the door, but he knew that the dog's brown eyes would be alight with joy. He could feel that long, hairy tail beating against his legs as Mutsy turned his attention to Sammy, licking his bare legs noisily.

'You two look like a pair of drowned rats! What happened?' Tom gave a snigger and even Jack had a grin on his face.

Alfie immediately asserted his authority. 'Tom, get a towel for Sammy. Get out something dry for him from the clothes box. Doesn't matter what. Jack, skin

15

that eel, slice down the back, clean out the innards and then pull the skin off. I've seen a fishmonger do that.'

'I'll fry it. Got a bit of suet left over. The butcher gave it to me with the sausages when I cleaned out his yard yesterday.' Jack took the eel from Sammy and seized a sharp knife from the cupboard. Alfie's father had been a cobbler and his tools still came in useful.

'Good,' said Alfie, pulling out a pair of ragged trousers from the box. They were even worse than the ones that he had on, but they would have to do until his own were dry. 'How much did you make, Tom, you and Mutsy?'

'Someone offered to buy Mutsy from me,' said Tom in an offhand way. 'Could have got a shilling for him.'

Alfie made no answer. Tom was just trying to annoy him, trying to get his temper to flare. Best to take no notice, he thought, rubbing himself vigorously, venting his anger on his own skin. Stupid, anyway, with Mutsy sitting there beside me! Expects me to make a fuss and tell him not to do such a thing, I suppose, thought Alfie, determined not to give his cousin the satisfaction of seeing him worried.

'Anyway, I got sixpence.' Tom sounded a little

disappointed that Alfie had not risen to his bait.

'Good,' said Alfie calmly. 'You'll be able to go out now and get some beer and some bread with that.'

When Tom looked away, Alfie bent down to give Mutsy an extra hug. The day when Mutsy had followed the gang home from Smithfield market had been one of the best days in Alfie's life. The big dog lived on rats, asked for nothing but affection and had made all of their lives more secure and more filled with fun. Tom was only teasing, he knew, but Alfie could not bear to think what life might be like without Mutsy.

'Here's Sarah. I see them black stockings of hers,' said Jack, peering up at the small window that showed the feet of the passers-by.

'Better get your trousers on, Alfie,' warned Tom. 'Sammy is decent now. Stick your arms into that coat, Sam. It'll do you for the moment. Your own things will be dry by the morning.'

'I'll let her in,' said Alfie, pulling up the trousers and fastening them with his usual piece of rope.

'What's that smell?' Sarah stopped at the doorway, her fingers pinching her nose. She was a small girl for twelve, short and thin with huge green eyes. She was dressed in the neat uniform of a scullery maid – black dress and white apron – and she worked during the day in a posh house in Bloomsbury and slept in a small room off the back kitchen of the house. Her evenings, however, were her own. Before the Ragged School had burnt down, she had spent them learning to read and write, but now she mostly came around to see the gang at Bow Street.

'Sammy and me have been in the river.'

'You should wash them clothes.' Sarah eyed the wet heap on the ground. 'It's no good just drying them. The stink will stay in them otherwise. Take them up to the pump at Bow Street, Alfie. Pump plenty of water over them. Squeeze them well out. I'd do it myself, but I daren't get my uniform dirty.'

Silently Alfie turned the coal sack inside out, shook out some of the coal dust and stuffed the clothes into it. His mind was still on the riverside scene.

'What happened to the two of you?' asked Sarah, looking from Alfie to Sammy.

'You tell her, Sammy, while I swill them things out.' Alfie moved quickly towards the doorway. 'Come on, Tom, you come too, and you can have that beer and see if you can get a nice loaf of newly baked bread to go alongside it. Don't get cheated by no stale stuff. These bakers are up to every trick.'

He kept on talking busily, either to Mutsy or to Tom, until he was through the door, up the steps and out into Bow Street. He parted from his cousin with a nod and strode down towards the pump, his faithful dog padding silently beside him. He was glad to be on his own for a while. He needed a little time to think.

Perhaps after supper was over and they all were full of fried eel, toast and hot beer, he would consult Sarah. She had a good, sharp brain and her opinion was always worth listening to.

What was the best thing to do? Common sense told him that it would be wisest to forget the whole matter. Why get himself mixed up with this? It was none of his business, he told himself as he pummelled and squeezed out the clothes. That's probably what Sarah would tell him.

But would it be the right thing to do? Or just the coward's way out?

By the time he returned with his sackful of wet clothes, he had reached his decision.

The fried eel was delicious – meaty and succulent – and the heated beer went very well with it. Alfie mopped the greasy juices from his plate with a piece of bread and took a long swallow of the beer that had been warming in his pewter mug on the iron grid over the fire.

'There was murder done today, Sarah,' he said casually. 'Joe, the chimney sweeping boy. Some geezer threw the body out of a gig onto the Hungerford Steps. I reckon someone should be caught for that. I've got a few ideas about tracking him down.'

Sarah listened carefully as Alfie went on, her green eyes wide, her face even paler than usual. She interrupted once to ask whether Alfie had seen the face of the man in the gig, nodding when Alfie said that he was too busy dragging Sammy through the river towards the boat. 'If I was you, Alfie,' she said when he had finished, 'I would have nothing to do with it. You don't want to get mixed up in no more murders.'

Alfie thought hard. There was sense in what she said. And then he thought of Joe and a feeling of anger welled up inside him. He rose to his feet decisively. 'I'm going to pop down to the police station and have a word with the inspector. Whoever the killer is, he's not going to get away with murder!'

CHAPTER 5

JUSTICE FOR JOE

'Friend of yours, was he?' PC Fairley sounded impatient.

'Not really. Just knew him to talk to.' Alfie kept his voice casual. PC Fairley was a new constable, an unpleasant fellow, always keen to twist your words.

'So he's nothing to you. Why come bothering me about it, then?'

Alfie said nothing. It was best not to contradict. He was beginning to be sorry that he had come. It couldn't help Joe.

'So he was a friend, was he?'

'Well, sort of,' said Alfie, trying to seem agreeable.

'On and off friends?'

Alfie nodded. What was he getting at?

'So you had a fight, did you?'

'No,' said Alfie calmly.

'You strangled him, is that what you're telling me? You squeezed his throat until you choked the life out of him. That was the way of it, wasn't it?' PC Fairley leant over his tall desk and thrust his face close to Alfie's.

'No, that's not what I'm telling you.' Alfie sighed impatiently. Was this man stupid? Or deaf?

'Tell me again,' said PC Fairley. 'Start at the beginning and tell it slowly because this time I'm going to write down every word that you say. That way, none of us can make any mistakes. Take your time. Remember, once you've said something, you can't go back on it.'

Slowly and carefully, Alfie went through how he and Sammy had found the body of the young chimney sweep by the riverside. He said that he believed Joe worked for Master Grimston, the chimney sweep, but he did not mention Joe's terror that morning and he said nothing, either, about Sammy's assertion that the body was flung from a gig.

Alfie was a little surprised to see how the constable

went on writing for quite some time after he had fallen silent. He felt scornful. He had had only a few months of learning to read and write at the Ragged School, but he could have taken the words down more quickly than that. However, he had enough sense to say nothing, so he just stood there gazing at the fire until the constable's quill had stopped scratching the paper.

'There you are then,' said PC Fairley, dusting a little sand over the wet ink on the page and then blowing it off. 'Now, I'm going to put some ink on the pen and then I want you to make your mark on the end of the page.' He drew a large X in the air. 'Can you do that for me?' he asked in a genial way.

'Yes, sir,' said Alfie. He'll get a shock when he sees that I write *Alfie Sykes* under it, he thought.

'Right, come around here now, can you reach? Yes, good lad. Just make the mark here.' The constable put a large, fat finger on a spot at the end of the closely-filled page.

Alfie reached up with the pen and then stopped. It was the sight of the lines and lines of writing that alerted him. Surely he had not said as much as that.

Curiously, he began to read it to himself.

I, Alfie Sykes, of Bow Street, Covent Garden,
do hereby declare that I did murder Joe the
chimney sweep . . .

'I didn't say that I killed him!' said Alfie angrily.
'What are you trying to put on me? I had nothing to
do with Joe's death. I —'

Then the constable's eyes flickered and he stood
up very straight. 'Oh, good evening, sir . . . Didn't see
you come in, sir.' He snatched the piece of paper from
Alfie, crumpled it and flung it into the fire.

Alfie swung round and saw a small man with
heavy eyebrows and sharp black eyes standing by the
door. It was Inspector Denham.

'Evening, Constable Fairley. Evening, Alfie. What
brings you here?' Alfie and his gang had helped the
inspector solve crimes in the past and had been well
rewarded for their efforts.

'Reporting the finding of a body to Constable
Fairley,' said Alfie. 'Found it about an hour ago, just
down by the water's edge by Hungerford Bridge.'
Constable Fairley, he thought, Constable *Unfairly*,
more like. Trying to pull a fast one on me. Trying to
make me sign a confession for the murder. But he
didn't bargain on me being able to read and write!

Alfie said nothing, however. The piece of paper had been burnt; there was no evidence now. *Least said, soonest mended*, his grandfather had always told him.

'A man?' queried the inspector.

'A boy – murdered, sir, this boy says.' PC Fairley put his hand in front of his mouth and said in a loud whisper, 'Some sort of a fight, I reckon. You know what these lads are like. Always at each other's throats.'

'Come in, Alfie.' Inspector Denham handed his coat and bowler hat to the police constable and walked into his office, followed by Alfie, who was careful not to look triumphantly at PC Fairley. Policemen, in Alfie's experience, could be dangerous. It paid to have them on your side and, if that was not possible, to avoid annoying them.

'Was that true about a fight?' asked Inspector Denham once the door was closed.

'No, sir, it wasn't true. I found him dead. Down by the river. By Hungerford Stairs.'

'Long dead?'

'No, sir, not long – still warm, not stiff nor nothing.'

Inspector Denham looked at Alfie carefully and Alfie looked back, trying not to appear defiant.

'To tell the truth, sir,' he blurted out, 'I'm sorry I

came. It won't do Joe no good.'

'Joe?' queried the inspector.

'Joe is . . . was his name. He was one of the chimney sweeping boys, worked for old Grimston the master chimney sweep.'

'I see. So if you think it's murder, who did it?'

'Don't know, sir. Can I go now, sir? I'd best be getting back home.'

Inspector Denham said nothing – he was a man of few words, thought Alfie fidgeting, rubbing first one foot, then the other, against the opposite leg. His feet were burning with chilblains – or perhaps it was frostbite: the water in the River Thames that afternoon had been cold enough to freeze the feet off any man.

'You said a minute ago that you were sorry you came here,' said the inspector, after a pause during which Alfie felt that his innermost thoughts were being read by the man behind the desk. 'Why did you come?'

Alfie looked at him in a puzzled way. He hadn't come for a reward; that was sure. No one would care about the death of a chimney sweep boy. There would be no reward for solving the murder of a poor boy like that. So why had he come?

'For Joe . . .' he said hesitantly.

'The body has come now, sir.' The sergeant stuck his head around the door after a perfunctory knock.

'Let's see. Come on, Alfie.' Inspector Denham got to his feet and Alfie followed him along the narrow corridor and into the cold, damp room where, under the harsh glare of the gas lamps, several bodies lay waiting to be identified.

One body looked very small. The inspector paused beside it, drew back the sheet and looked at Alfie, who gulped then nodded silently. That was Joe, in all his dirt, and, yes, he had been murdered. There could be no other reason for that purple protruding tongue.

'So you did it for Joe,' mused Inspector Denham, replacing the sheet over the dead boy's face. 'I think I know what you mean, Alfie. You want justice for Joe, that's right, isn't it?'

Alfie nodded again and swallowed hard. If Joe was to have justice then he would have to tell all that he knew. And in that moment he clearly saw the dangers that lay ahead. Out there on the streets of London was the man who had murdered Joe. A man in a gig, a man who had seen two boys beside the body. A man who must now be wondering whether he had been seen throwing the body out towards the river. If Alfie told the police about the man in the gig, it was more likely that the man would be able to track him and Sammy down.

Should he do it?

'Are you scared?' asked the inspector, looking at him narrowly. Once again he removed the sheet.

Alfie looked down at the dead boy's face. He took a long moment before he spoke. 'No, sir,' he said loudly. 'I'm not scared. Takes a lot to scare Alfie Sykes. I'll track down that geezer who did this to poor old Joe.'

He was lying, of course. He knew that he had good reason to be scared.

A man who had killed once would not hesitate to kill again.

CHAPTER 6

UNRAVELLING
A MYSTERY

Alfie found it hard to stop thinking about Joe the next day. He wasn't sure whether Inspector Denham had believed him or not about the gig and what Joe had said. He had listened and said very little, telling Alfie to come and see him again if he found out any more about the death of the chimney sweeper.

That afternoon, Alfie got ready to take Sammy to the entrance of Covent Garden Theatre.

'We'll leave these very torn trousers on you, Sam,' he said, 'and that old coat. Let's give your face a wash, though, and I'll comb your hair. Sarah made a good job of washing it last night. What we want is to get all them toffs thinking you're a good boy just like their children, but you're very poor. Then they'll give you some of their change and they'll feel good, like it's Christmas come early!'

'Let's take Mutsy too, and then you and he can do a duet,' suggested Tom. The rich children always laughed when Sammy hit the high note and Mutsy joined in with a high-pitched wail.

'That's a good idea,' said Alfie. And then he thought of poor Joe again. He would leave Sammy with Tom and go to Hungerford Market to see if any of the stallholders had seen anything the afternoon of Joe's death.

'Yesterday, round about three o' clock?' said Lizzie the stallholder. Her stall was on the very edge of Hungerford market, just beside the road going down to the river. Alfie had chosen her stall for that reason and was happy for a wage of two pence to scrub the potatoes while Lizzie baked and sold them. Lizzie was sharp and might have spotted the gig – she might even have an idea who drove it.

'Didn't see no gig with one man in it, though – not as I can remember, anyways. Why are you asking?' she demanded sharply.

'This toff says he'll give me a penny for holding his horse, goes off for half an hour and then comes back and drives off without a farthing for my trouble,' lied Alfie glibly.

'Nothing you can do about it now,' said Lizzie with a sigh. 'One law for the rich and one law for us. That's life, Alfie.' Then she paused. 'No, I tell a lie,' she said dramatically. 'I remember now. I did see a gig, came along ever so fast. Shouted at someone with a cart to get out of his way or he'd see him hauled up in front of the court.'

'Toff, was he?' enquired Alfie, listening with interest. 'Sounds like a toff.' Toffs, in his experience, were very likely to shout at people and threaten them with the law.

'Not sure,' said Lizzie, her black eyebrows drawn together while she searched her memory. 'Perhaps he was, but he was a bit rough for a toff. Bit of a lunatic, if you ask me. Screamed out laughing when an old man slipped in the mud while he was trying to get out of the way.'

There was a long queue outside the door to Covent Garden Theatre when Alfie got back. Sammy, Tom and Mutsy were standing under one of the arches to the square. Sammy had stopped singing; the doors would open at any minute.

'How did you do?' asked Alfie, rubbing his cold hands through Mutsy's warm fur.

'Good,' said Tom. 'Eleven pence. We'd better be getting home now, I was just saying to Sammy. It's getting colder every minute.'

'Be snow, soon, I wouldn't be surprised. I smell it.' Sammy sniffed the air as if he were a dog himself.

Alfie looked around. 'More likely rain,' he began and then stopped. Sammy was right. First one icy snowflake drifted down and then another. The children in the queue screamed with excitement. Men and women came out of the shops and turned their faces to the sky.

'Sammy,' said Alfie, watching the flakes begin to settle on the wet roof of the market, 'do you remember that song that you learnt from Grandad – all about stars and snow and all that?'

Sammy did not reply. A look of concentration came over his face, then he nodded.

'Wait until I bring you to the top of the queue,' said Alfie. 'Tom, you bring that bowl, but don't hold it out until I give you the nod.'

The snow had begun to fall heavily. The children

were beginning to shiver. Sammy's voice rose up high and clear.

Only when Sammy reached the last words about the poor children shivering in the snow did Alfie nod to Tom to walk along the line with the bowl. Even some of the people who had already given money walked back to slip some more change into Tom's bowl.

'Two whole pounds of sausages for tonight, Jack old son! And two pints of that small beer.' Alfie was exploding with their success. He led Sammy to the fire, piled on some more coal, saw Mutsy sink down on his brother's cold feet and then, quite suddenly, thought of Joe again. He had to find out what was happening.

'Be back in a few ticks,' he said as he went to the door.

'I've no news for you, Alfie,' said Inspector Denham. He beckoned to Alfie to come into his private office and shut the door before continuing.

'I sent a man around to Goodwin's Court this morning, where Joe was working that day, but we got nothing useful. Just one old lady lives by herself in

Number Four, a Mrs Leamington. As far as Grimston, the master chimney sweep, is concerned, the boy just disappeared. He went up the chimney in the morning and never came back. Grimston dropped him off and went to Leicester Square with another couple of boys. When he came back to pick up Joe, there was no sign of him and no one in the house had seen anything of him either.'

'So what did Mr Grimston do then?' Alfie put in the question as Inspector Denham had fallen silent and was staring at the opposite wall with an odd look on his face.

'Just went home, apparently,' said Inspector Denham. 'He told the constable that he often lost chimney sweeping boys – and anyway Joe was getting a bit too big for some of the chimneys so he didn't really care if he saw him again or not.'

Once more there was that odd look, almost as though he were angry about something. Alfie stared curiously at him. Respectable people didn't usually seem to bother themselves too much about poor children.

'Apparently he told the scullery maid to light all of the fires before her mistress came home.' The words seemed to explode with fury from Inspector Denham.

'That's what he does, this man Grimston! Burns out the boys! Calls himself a good Christian!' Inspector Denham went to the door and called, 'Constable, come in here a minute. Tell me what that . . . what the master chimney sweep said.'

PC Fairley dug in his pocket, gave Alfie a look, then produced a notebook, gave Alfie another look and read aloud. 'Some of these boys gets too comfortable. They falls asleep. There's just one way to get them out. We just lights a fire and then they pop out of the chimney as fast as lightning. It always works, it does . . . as long as they's still alive, of course.'

PC Fairley closed his notebook and looked enquiringly at Inspector Denham.

'Thank you, Constable.'

Alfie waited until the door shut to speak; he had a funny feeling that he had to comfort the inspector. 'But Joe wasn't burnt to death, was he, sir? He was strangled. Someone choked the life out of him with a pair of hands.'

CHAPTER 7

ALFIE
TAKES A CHANCE

'Goodwin's Court!' said Sarah sharply. 'Not Number Four?'

'That's right,' said Alfie, looking at her curiously.

Inspector Denham had told him that the old lady had gone to her daughter's house the night before Joe was killed, so that her fires could be left unlit until the chimneys had been cleaned. This left the three women servants at home – the cook, the parlour maid and the scullery maid. But why should any of them murder Joe?

What had Joe seen that day? Alfie wished that he could remember his words better. A bend . . . the wrong way . . . being scared?

'Alfie, are you listening to me?' Sarah sounded exasperated and Alfie shook his head, trying to shake out the words spoken by the dead boy.

'Yeah, I'm listening,' he said.

'I was trying to tell you that I know the scullery maid there, Ellen. She was at the foundling hospital at Coram Fields with me. We were both trained as scullery maids at the same time and we got jobs the same week. I haven't seen much of her since, but sometimes we meet when we're sent out for vegetables from Covent Garden. I went back to Goodwin's Court once with her when she couldn't carry all her shopping herself. I met the cook – Mrs . . . something beginning with B . . . Bailey, I think.'

Alfie was on his feet in a moment. 'Could you take me round there, Sarah? I'd like to see that house, talk to the servants, find out what's going on there. Joe saw something that scared the living daylights out of him. We could go now and I'll walk back home with you afterwards.' He hesitated for a moment and then looked across at his brother. Sammy was a good person to have nearby during a conversation. He could hear things – things that had not been said, like fear or anger – and he could sense when someone was lying.

'All right if Sammy comes too?' he asked. 'Could do with a bit of a walk, couldn't you, Sam? You've been indoors all day.'

The day had been freezing with a bitter north wind that swept around corners and straight through the boys' ragged clothes. Alfie had begun to regret spending all that money on the sausages, which were nearly all gone already. In weather like this, no one wanted to hang around watching a boy doing tricks or singing, so it was hard to earn anything on the streets. Alfie had gone down to the river to help Jack with the coal and sent Tom to scrub potatoes for Lizzie at Hungerford market, but by midday they had all given up and come home. The river was too icy even for Jack, and not even baked potatoes were selling on this terrible day.

So the boys had spent the afternoon teaching Mutsy some new tricks. Alfie had made a sign that said, *MUTSY, CHAMPION OF THE SUMS*.

Tom called out the numbers. 'Two and two,' he shouted, and Mutsy gave four short barks. 'Three and three,' he said, and Mutsy gave six barks. By the end of the afternoon Mutsy could do six sums and was so excited at all the praise he got that he started to tear round and round the small cellar, leaping over the tatty old cushions and the boys. When Sarah had arrived, he went through the whole performance again for her.

Once Mutsy had calmed down, Alfie had told Sarah what Inspector Denham had said about Goodwin's Court and the old lady being away, and she'd recognised the address.

'So it's the servants that we have to look at,' said Sarah. 'Ellen's not a murderer, though, and the cook seemed nice enough . . .'

'Or old Master Grimston himself,' said Jack.

'Don't make sense, though, do it?' argued Alfie. 'Why should he murder Joe? He's got no reason to. If he didn't like him, he could just sack him.'

'Perhaps Joe found out something about Master Grimston,' suggested Tom. 'Maybe there was a dead body in the chimney!'

'Stupid!' said Alfie with annoyance. Tom was interrupting his thoughts.

'He's got something, though, Alfie,' said Sarah. 'Why should they call the sweep in December? In our house, the sweep comes in summer, when the fire's not being used.' She narrowed her eyes as she thought. 'The only time I can remember a sweep being called during the winter was when the smoke wasn't going up the chimney properly – and they found that the last sweeping boy had left half a broom head in the chimney.'

'See!' said Tom triumphantly. 'There's something up the chimney!'

'We'd better be going,' said Alfie, ignoring him. It was pointless trying to guess. Surely Sarah's friend, Ellen, would be able to tell them why the sweep had been called in December.

Goodwin's Court was a small alleyway off St Martin's Lane, too narrow for any traffic to pass down it. It was lit by three large gas lamps and lined on both sides by a terrace of old-fashioned brick houses. Each house was three storeys high, with black-framed, bow-fronted windows on the ground floor, tall eight-paned windows on the first floor and small, square windows at the top. The servants probably slept up there, thought Alfie, looking up.

'We can't just knock on the front door,' whispered Sarah in his ear. 'We'll have to go round the back and find the kitchen entrance.'

Alfie looked at the neat black-painted door with a gold number four, gold knocker, gold knob and gold letterbox, and decided that she was right. Front doors were for toffs, not for people like them. But suddenly the door opened and a stout, middle-aged woman wearing a snowy white apron appeared, followed by a well-dressed little old lady.

'Wait in the warmth while I find a cab for you, ma'am,' the woman in the apron was saying.

Alfie acted fast. 'Call you a cab, ma'am?' he said quickly and sped back up towards St Martin's Lane as soon as he received a nod. He was in luck. There was a cab sauntering along St Martin's Lane. Alfie stuck two fingers into his mouth and gave a piercing whistle and the horse stopped almost before the man had time to pull the reins.

'Fare for you down there. I'll hold the horse.' Alfie was brisk. A little business on the side was always welcome – he might earn a penny.

When the cabman came back, carefully matching his step to the old lady's, he winked at Alfie. 'Good lad, ain't he, madam?' he said, and she smiled sweetly and gave Alfie a sixpence before getting into the cab.

Nice old lady, he thought as he bolted back down the alleyway.

Sarah was talking to the stout woman in the apron at the front door of Number Four, as Sammy stood by silently. 'And here is Alfie, who just helped your mistress find a cab,' she said nervously.

'Well . . .' the cook was saying, looking up and down the street with a frown, 'I suppose you might as well come in this way, now Mrs Leamington has left. Quickly, now, while no one's around! Ellen's in the kitchen. Now wipe your feet carefully on that mat. There's only three of us here in the house to do all the work so we don't want no mess.'

The cook sounded a bit bad-tempered, thought Alfie, so he snatched off his cap and Sammy's, made an exaggerated show of cleaning his bare feet and helping Sammy to do the same. She seemed to be softened by the sight of Sammy and said more affably, 'Come in and get warm, all of you.'

She opened the door at the far end of the hallway and then clicked her tongue with annoyance.

'Drat that chimney,' she said. 'It's still smoking.'

CHAPTER 8

THE BLOCKED CHIMNEY

Alfie was never one to miss an opportunity. Dropping Sammy's arm instantly, he crossed the polished brick tiles and knelt down in front of the kitchen fire, ignoring the cloud of smoke that puffed out into his face. Cautiously he moved his head in over the small fire and looked up the chimney, then stood back with a grave face. The two women and the girl were all staring at him. He saw the girl – that must be Ellen – raise her eyebrows at Sarah and Sarah gave her a reassuring nod. Sammy sat quietly by Sarah with the usual calm expression on his face.

Carefully Alfie picked up a kitchen chair, carried it

over to the fireplace, stood on it, tapped the warm chimney breast two or three times in different places, nodded solemnly to himself, then got down. He gently replaced the chair to its place under the table before turning to face Mrs Bailey.

'I know what your problem is, ma'am,' he said respectfully. 'A brick has come loose and that's blocking the chimney.'

'Oh no,' exclaimed the cook. 'Don't say we have to go through all that again! Get that Grimston, again? The third time this winter! We've had enough trouble already, haven't we, Mavis?'

'Shocking,' said Mavis the parlour maid, her lips pursed and her nose tilted as though there was a bad smell under it. 'Policemen coming around here and asking questions!'

'Poor little boy!' sighed Ellen. She was a tall, thin girl with sad eyes that overflowed now at the thought of the death of the last chimney sweeper.

'Nothing to do with us, Ellen,' snapped Mavis. 'I told you, stop talking about that. It upsets the missus. I don't want to hear another word about it.' She glared around and then said impatiently, 'Well, the missus won't be pleased if I tell her that we have to get the sweep back again.'

'Another day with no fires,' groaned Mrs Bailey.

Alfie made himself wait. Just as well if they had time to think of how uncomfortable it was when the sweep came – no heat, no cooked food, no hot water for their cups of tea.

'I might be able to help you,' he said after a minute.

'You?' Mavis looked at him scornfully.

'Would you?' asked Mrs Bailey at the same moment.

'No problem,' said Alfie grandly. 'My grandfather was a chimney sweep and he taught me to do a good job on our chimney at home.' His grandfather had actually been a street singer but neither Sarah nor Sammy was going to reveal that. Sammy sat placidly in front of the fire and Sarah examined the fingernails of her right hand.

'How long would it take?' The cook's question popped out immediately. She sounded keen.

'Wouldn't take long. I'd come in early – about five or six in the morning and be all finished by the time that you want to get the breakfast.'

'That would work,' said the cook thoughtfully. 'Not tomorrow. What about you coming here on Friday morning? Would that suit you?'

Mavis stared at her with horror. 'You wouldn't trust a boy off the street, would you, Mrs Bailey?'

'Suits me if it suits you,' said Alfie, ignoring the parlour maid. He stuck out his hand to the cook. 'Alfie Sykes at your service, ma'am. Chimneys brushed, knives cleaned, yards scrubbed. Anything you want; just ask.'

'Pleased to meet you, Alfie,' said Mrs Bailey with a giggle. 'And tell me about this young man?' She glanced over at Sammy.

'Sammy is Alfie's brother,' said Sarah.

'How about a bit of nice apple cake?' asked Mrs Bailey. 'Come on, Mavis, get that apple cake from the pantry. Missus won't want any more of it. She don't eat much. Got no appetite. She's too worried about that son of hers, poor soul.'

'He's lucky to have a mother,' said Alfie with a heavy sigh. 'Me and Sammy don't have none.' He watched as Mavis, with a sour expression on her face, came in from the pantry with a large round apple cake. Only a few slices were taken from it. 'Sammy,' he ordered, 'sing that song that Mother liked, the one about her watching your infant bed.'

So Sammy sang the song and Mrs Bailey sighed and said that young Mr Leamington, the old lady's son, should have been there to listen and then he might appreciate his mother better.

After that, Mavis flounced off, saying that she had work to do and she didn't like apple cake much anyway. Ellen put plates and knives on the table. Mrs Bailey poured out large mugs of milk and a cup of tea for herself and they all sat around the fire cosily, batting away the odd puff of smoke, while Mrs Bailey told them all about the old lady's son.

'He's coming to dinner again tomorrow night,' she said with a heavy sigh. 'He'll be at the same business, again, asking the missus for money. On and on, like water dripping on stone, that's the way that Mr Arthur is. She hasn't too much for herself, poor old thing. Can't afford a carriage or a manservant, but he never sees that. It's pester, pester, pester with him. He's a bad lot.'

'Why doesn't he get a job?' asked Sarah.

'He's too idle, dear, that's the truth of the matter. He went to a good school and all, but he was a spoilt child, young Mr Arthur, and now he's a spoilt man. Money is his god. He has the best of everything while she goes without. He has to have his own horse and his fancy gig, of course, but she has to call a cab when she visits anyone. Oh well, it's none of my business.' Alfie's sharp brain registered the fact that young Mr Leamington owned a gig, as Mrs Bailey heaved a long sigh and added, 'He never even listens to her when she tries to talk to him. He even turned up quite early the day that the sweep was here, even though she had told him forty times that she would be staying with his sister.'

'Perhaps he came to help,' suggested Alfie with a grin. Another piece of information to store in his mind. So Arthur Leamington was around on the day that the sweep was at Goodwin's Court – that was interesting. He looked at Sarah and saw the same thought cross her mind.

'Perhaps he wanted to talk to Master Grimston, see that he did a good job,' put in Sarah.

'Not him, dear, he has no interest in making life easy for his mother. No, he probably just came to borrow money. He cleared off quickly as soon as he saw what was going on. Left that gig of his in the yard, though. Probably went off to the Red Lion and then came back and collected the gig. It was gone when I looked next.'

'We'd better be getting along now,' said Alfie, seeing that the cake had been finished and the fire was beginning to die down. 'We want to see Sarah home before it's too late. Too many drunk men around!'

'It's a terrible thing, that, drink!' sighed Mrs Bailey. 'It's ruined Mr Arthur! Well, goodbye all of you and we'll see you on Friday morning, Alfie.'

'Alfie,' said Sarah as they walked up St Martin's Lane, 'do you think that this Arthur Leamington could have anything to do with Joe's death?'

'Can't see why,' said Alfie doubtfully. 'What good would it do him to murder a poor sweeping boy?'

'He has a gig,' said Sammy quietly. 'And it was here on Monday morning.'

'I know,' said Alfie. 'It's just that I can't think of any possible reason for Arthur Leamington to murder a sweeping boy.'

'I reckon we should be hanging around tomorrow when he arrives for his supper,' Sammy went on. 'I'd know the sound of that gig again.' He paused, then added, 'I can just hear the sound of the horse's hoofs and the rattle of that wheel when the body of poor old Joe was thrown out towards the water.'

'You're right,' said Alfie. 'We'll do that. One step at a time. If it is the same gig then we can start poking around to find a motive.'

And he tried to put from his mind the possibility that the driver of the gig would recognise the two boys who had bent over the dead body of Joe the chimney sweep.

CHAPTER 9

A BODY
ON A SLAB

'You Alfie Sykes?' The policeman was coming down the steps to the cellar when Alfie opened the door in the morning.

'That's right,' said Alfie, feeling slightly alarmed. He didn't recognise the man.

'You're wanted at Bow Street police station – Inspector Denham would like a word.' And with that the constable marched on down Bow Street towards Long Acre.

Rather apprehensively Alfie made his way towards the blue light shining through the early morning fog.

Inspector Denham was already inside, striding up

and down the stone floor, arms crossed and hands slapping his sides.

'Freezing morning,' he said when Alfie slid in through the door.

'Yes, sir,' agreed Alfie. He couldn't quite see why the inspector was so cold with his big woollen overcoat and his heavy boots. He should try bare feet and rags, Alfie thought and saw the same thought cross the inspector's mind. He stopped pacing and looked at Alfie's feet.

'Here's half a crown for you,' he said abruptly, delving into his pocket. 'Buy yourself a pair of boots. You make me cold to look at you. And take that handkerchief and blow your nose. All that sniffing is stopping me thinking.'

'Thank you, sir,' said Alfie, giving his nose a good blow and stuffing the fine linen handkerchief into his sleeve, in response to a gesture from the inspector to keep it. He pocketed the coin with the other hand, feeling rather amazed. Half a crown would buy one pair of boots all right, but what about the rest of the gang? He couldn't wear boots and have them go barefoot. Perhaps they could all share them. In truth, he would have preferred to put the money aside for rent and food, but it would be embarrassing to appear in front of the inspector with bare feet from now on.

'Come into my office,' said Inspector Denham. 'It's even colder than this place but it's quieter.' He glared at the two constables who were chatting by the window.

'This Mr Grimston,' said the inspector, shutting the door behind him, 'do you know him at all?'

'A bit,' said Alfie. He had never even spoken to Master Grimston, but with Inspector Denham he generally pretended to have more knowledge than he actually possessed. Inspector Denham was generous; he paid well for help.

'The police doctor confirmed that Joe was strangled. Didn't take much strength, according to the doctor. Anyone could have done it. Throat and lungs already stuffed with soot.'

Alfie nodded. 'Not surprised,' he said. 'Lots of them chimney sweeping boys die in their beds, choked up with the soot. Not that Grimston would give them a bed – more likely a heap of straw.'

'That's right,' agreed the inspector. 'We often see Grimston here at Bow Street magistrates' court. Comes to give evidence at inquests into those deaths. But this case is different. Any ideas who could have done it?'

Alfie shook his head. 'No, sir,' he said. He had told the inspector all about the man in the gig, and about the words spoken by Joe when he had met him early that morning. 'How long had he been dead, sir?' he asked.

'Only a couple of hours, according to the police surgeon.'

'I thought that; the body wasn't cold when I felt it.' Alfie nodded with satisfaction. He liked to get these things right. 'Killed not long before he was dumped, I suppose,' he continued. 'He'd probably finished his work and was waiting on the pavement or something.'

'According to Grimston, he had arranged to pick up the boy at the yard to the back of the house. He had a job for him at a public house in Long Acre, but Joe wasn't there, so he picked up another boy for that job – then went back to Goodwin's Court and got the scullery maid to light the fires.' The inspector frowned. 'I've had men questioning everyone in the neighbourhood, and no one laid eyes on the boy after early that morning. It's a mystery.'

Inspector Denham rattled the poker in the fire again. He wasn't doing it much good, but he didn't seem to be noticing. 'I keep thinking that this death must be something to do with that man Grimston,' he said with his back turned to Alfie – almost as though he was speaking to himself. And then, in an even lower tone, added, 'I wouldn't mind seeing that man in the dock . . .'

Alfie didn't reply. He wasn't meant to reply, he decided. But was Grimston responsible for the death of Joe? He had said himself that Grimston had no reason to kill Joe, but perhaps he got angry with the boy for some reason? What if Joe had said that he didn't want to do another job, that he was tired or something, and Grimston had put his hands around the boy's neck and choked the life out of him?

It seemed unlikely that Joe would argue but it wouldn't take much for Grimston to get into one of his rages. Alfie had heard him scream and shout at the boys, and Joe was terrified of him. The only trouble was that Grimston drove a cart, not a gig, and Sammy had said it was a gig he heard down by the river. Alfie wasn't so sure, though he was certain that a gig came towards them after they had found the body. But perhaps that gig had nothing to do with the murder? Perhaps it was just someone driving along beside the river towards Waterloo Bridge who decided that the fog was getting too bad and then turned back. But Sammy had heard a gig and had heard something being thrown out of the gig and Sammy was usually right. However, Grimston's cart was only a two-wheeled, one-horse affair – surely it couldn't sound so different from a gig? Alfie put the puzzle away from him for the moment.

'Anyone talk to the sweeping boys, sir?' he asked.

'Couldn't get anything out of them, frightened to death, poor little beggars.' The inspector gave the fire one last poke and then turned around. 'I wondered about you, Alfie. They might talk to you. You might get something out of them.' He threw the poker down on the hearth with a clatter. 'Don't take any risks, though. That Grimston is a nasty piece of work. The life of a boy wouldn't mean much to him. He goes through boys the way I go through cigars. Use one up and then get another one.'

Alfie nodded. He agreed with the inspector but thought that he was probably a match for Master Grimston. He could easily trick the old monster. Perhaps he could ask about a job – no, that wouldn't work. Alfie knew he was much too big for a chimney sweeping boy.

'I'll come up with a story – something about a little brother needing a job . . .' He grinned at the inspector, but to his surprise the man did not smile back.

'Be careful, Alfie,' he said with emphasis. 'He's a dangerous man. Don't let him see what you're up to. I don't want to come in one morning and find your body lying on one of those marble slabs.'

CHAPTER 10

A DANGEROUS MAN

Grimston lodged his boys in a place known as Devil's Acre, behind Westminster Abbey. His chimney sweeping boys slept in a stable there, according to poor Joe, but when Alfie found the place eventually as the evening was beginning to draw in, he thought that it wasn't fit for any decent kind of horse.

Hundreds of years ago, this had been a fine house with stables and a courtyard attached, but damp from the river and the action of beetles had rotted and worn down the timber, causing one side of the house to slip down into the mire beneath it. There was a large pool of stagnant water in front of it and behind was a row of tumbledown stables with crumbling walls and gaping holes in the roofs. In the worst of these, Grimston housed his chimney sweeping boys.

Alfie waited patiently and eventually a cart turned in through the gap where once there had been a gate. Alfie took from his pocket the large, white handkerchief given to him by Inspector Denham and flourished it in front of his nose. Tom, standing in front of a doorway opposite, nodded and strolled off.

'Evening,' said Alfie, stepping forward when Grimston stopped the cart.

Grimston gave him one uninterested look, then glanced over his shoulder and barked 'Out!' at the soot-covered boys in the back of the cart. They climbed out and scuttled like rats across to the crumbling stable. There were only three of them – Grimston normally kept four boys – and all were even smaller and thinner than Joe.

'What do you want?' Grimston did not stir from the cart, but glared down impatiently at Alfie. Obviously neither he nor his horse was going to spend the night in Devil's Acre.

'Heard you might be looking for a chimney sweeping boy?' Alfie had washed his face and combed his hair. He wore his least ragged clothes and the new boots and tried to look and sound older, deepening his voice.

'What of it?'

'My old man married again,' said Alfie, who had his story well established in his mind. 'His new lady had a five-year-old lad. Now she's croaked it – the fever. My father don't want the boy. We're looking for a good apprenticeship for him – he's six now – we want someone who could take him off our hands.'

'Not sure . . . I'm fussy about the boys I take on. Don't want no one coming around and asking questions and wanting to tell the kid a bedtime story. If I take on a boy, that's that. No interference.'

'Suits us.' Alfie stretched his mouth in a grin. 'What happened to your last boy? The soot, was it?'

'No.' Grimston had a husky voice and it was hard to make out whether he was puzzled or not. 'Don't know what happened to him, to be honest. Picked up dead, he was, lying next to the river by Hungerford Steps. Beats me what he was doing down there!'

Alfie listened with interest. Did the man sound angry, guilty or just puzzled? From the corner of his eye, he saw Tom leading Sammy by the arm. They positioned themselves on the pavement just where the cart would pass on the way out of the stable yard.

Earlier on they had left Sammy in Westminster Abbey listening to the church choir and organ; Alfie had not wanted Grimston to connect Sammy with him. The blind boy was well known around Westminster Abbey and someone was bound to know who he was and perhaps connect Alfie with Inspector Denham. On the other hand, only Sammy would be able to tell whether Grimston's cart was the vehicle he had heard on the night of the murder.

'Anyway,' said Grimston, 'I'm off now. You get your father to come around with the boy tomorrow – same time, about; same place anyway. Six years old, did you say? Not too big, is he?'

'He's not been used to too much feeding since his mother died.' Alfie tried a chuckle.

'Might suit me.' Grimston shook the reins of the horse and he moved off through the gateway.

Alfie listened intently. A light cart; the wheels moved well and smoothly. He couldn't hear anything to indicate that one was loose, but then Sammy could hear things that no one else could. He waited until the cart had disappeared.

He was just about to join Tom and Sammy when a maidservant came out from the Mitre & Dove public house. The heavy bucket she carried dragged one of her shoulders down. As she came through the archway Alfie sauntered over towards her. 'Carry your bucket, ma'am?' He gave her a smile.

She looked him up and down without interest. 'You can if you like,' she said. 'It's just for them chimney sweeping boys over there. Here take it – I've got to be off. We're that busy tonight. Just dump the bucket down in front of them and leave it. I collect the empty bucket in the morning when they're gone off to work.'

Just as though they were a crowd of little pigs, thought Alfie, picking up the bucket that the girl had left on the ground. By the gas lamp at the gateway he could see that the contents of the bucket looked like pig-swill too. Just a foul-smelling mess of leftovers from plates, burnt bits from saucepans and mouldy slices of bread.

'Here you are, lads,' he said as he came to the door. It was pitch dark in there and he waited until they came out before putting down the bucket.

They seemed surprised to see him, but they plunged their hands into the mess and began stuffing it into their mouths as fast as it would go.

'Nice, was it?' asked Alfie when the bucket had been cleared.

'Gets the soot out of your throat,' said one of them hoarsely.

They were shivering and the fog was coming down heavily. The damp air from the swamp by the river smelt bad – almost as though the smell itself would bring fever. Alfie did not fancy hanging around there too long.

'What happened to Joe?' he asked abruptly.

'Don't know,' said one and the words were echoed by the other two.

By the dim light from the gas lamp, Alfie could just see the whites of their eyes, framed by the black faces and soot-encrusted hair. They were scared; there was no doubt about that.

'Got his throat massaged a bit too much by Master Grimston, was that it?' Alfie tried another laugh and the boys looked at each other. The smallest of the three began to cry.

'Shut up!' hissed a slightly larger boy. He aimed a mixture of spit and black soot in the direction of Alfie's shiny new boots.

'We don't know nothing,' sobbed the smallest one and then he began to cough violently. He sank to his knees, still coughing, and the oldest boy bent over him.

'Clear off; you're upsetting my brother.' He glared

at Alfie and there was a look of terrible fear in his eyes as he held the child under his armpits and tried to get him to stand up.

Alfie watched in silence. The small boy was bone thin with bowed shoulders and a chest hardly bigger than an infant's. It seemed as though the fit of coughing would never cease – that the boy would die in front of his eyes. He tried to help by patting the child on the back – he dimly remembered his mother doing that to Tom when he had a winter cough – but it didn't seem to do much.

'Clear off,' repeated the oldest boy. 'We've told you – we know nothing.'

'And Master tells us to answer no questions,' added the second boy.

Alfie gave one last look at the youngest boy. He had dropped to the ground again, exhausted by his coughing fit. The other boys bent down and dragged him inside the broken-down stable. There was no doubt in Alfie's mind that the boys had been terrified into concealing something.

'Well?' he asked when he joined Sammy and Tom.

'Not the same thing at all,' said Sammy. 'Why didn't you listen to me? I told you it was a gig! I'd know a gig from a cart any day.'

Alfie grinned. Sammy had come up with the goods as usual. A court of law might not take his evidence, but Alfie was pretty sure now that Joe's body wasn't thrown down by the river from Master Grimston's cart.

But why had the sweeping boys looked at each other like that?

What were they scared of?

CHAPTER 11

SARAH LISTENS

'That's the parlour maid – looks like she's going out for the evening,' said Alfie in a low voice. He, Sammy and Sarah were waiting for the arrival of Arthur Leamington's gig near the back entrance to Number Four, in the narrow street where the horses for Goodwin's Court were stabled.

'That's right,' agreed Sarah. 'She's all dolled up – I like that hat!'

'They'll be short-handed tonight if the old lady is having her son to dinner,' said Alfie shrewdly. 'Sarah, why don't you —'

'— offer to help?' finished Sarah. 'That's an idea. I'll

tell the cook that sometimes I wait at table.' She looked all around before saying in a low voice, 'That would give me a chance to have a look at Mr Leamington.'

Alfie nodded. He still couldn't see why Mr Leamington, the son of the old lady at Number Four Goodwin's Court, should kill Joe, but he did have a gig and he was connected with the house where Joe was last seen alive, and he had been seen at the house on the day that Joe was murdered.

'You go and knock on the back door,' he said to Sarah. 'Sammy and I will go and wait in the entrance to Goodwin's Court until the gig arrives.'

Only a few minutes passed before Sammy turned an alert face towards St Martin's Lane.

'Cab,' he said.

Alfie looked. A horse-drawn cab had stopped on the main road – no cabs came down this narrow street. A young man wearing a shiny top hat got out and handed his fare to the cab-driver. He laughed at a remark from the cabbie – a strange, high-pitched laugh – and tossed a coin to him. Then he walked lightly towards Goodwin's Court, swinging his cane as he went.

Alfie watched carefully and then groaned. 'Yeah,' he said with disgust, 'that's him just gone by us, I reckon. That's the son, Mr Leamington. Didn't bring his gig, tonight . . . Isn't that just our luck!'

'Could be interesting,' said Sammy thoughtfully.

'Interesting! Is that all you can say?' Alfie growled.

'No good you getting mad,' replied Sammy placidly. 'Use your head. Why should a man that owns his own gig go to the trouble of getting a cab?'

'Horse lame?' said Alfie.

'Could be,' admitted Sammy, 'but it could be that he was afraid that the gig might get him tied into the murder. If I was a toff who'd done a murder and I thought I might have been seen in this gig, well, I'd give it a rest for a week or so and get a cab – wouldn't you?'

Alfie slapped his brother on the back and gave a laugh. He was just about to reply when the sound of his own laugh reminded him of something. 'Did you hear him laugh, Sammy?' he asked. 'Could you do it for me? I want to remember that laugh. It sounded funny.'

'Bit like a horse neighing,' agreed Sammy. He stood still for a moment, just as though he were looking into himself, and then produced an exact copy of Mr Leamington's laugh.

'I'll know that laugh again,' said Alfie. 'You know

Lizzie at the Hungerford market – the one that sells the baked potatoes? Well, she said something about the man in the gig having a funny laugh.'

'I just wondered if you needed any help since you were having a dinner party tonight?' said Sarah.

Mrs Bailey the cook looked her up and down from her trim shoes to her clean apron and tidy hair and then gave a welcoming smile.

'Well, you're a sight for sore eyes,' she said cordially. 'That Mavis has taken herself off. Wouldn't change her evening out for anything. Oh no, not her. Didn't care if Mr Leamington was coming to supper or not. "Missus should have remembered that it was my night out."' The cook held her nose high in the air and mimicked Mavis.

Sarah laughed. 'I can wait at table if you like,' she offered. 'I've done it once or twice when the parlour maid wasn't there in Bloomsbury Square. I know what to do. That's if Ellen doesn't mind.'

'Ellen's too shy to wait at table,' said the cook decisively. 'Come on, you can borrow Mavis's cap and lace-trimmed apron. It will make you look the real thing. It's a good thing that you turned up. I was even thinking of asking Number Eleven if they could spare someone but I didn't like to – it's not as if Missus is friendly with them. Of course, Number Five, she's great friends with them – but they've been in Italy for most of the year.'

By the time that Sarah entered the dining room, she was confident that she looked the part. Mavis's cap and apron looked good on her and Mrs Leamington gave her an encouraging smile. However, her son looked impatient and that disconcerted Sarah as she stationed herself beside Mr Leamington and filled the ladle from the soup tureen.

'Soup, sir?' enquired Sarah in a low voice. In spite of her efforts, it shook a little with nerves. At the last moment, she wondered whether it was correct for her to be on the man's left side. He didn't say anything, just gave an impatient nod, so she carefully ladled the steaming liquid into his bowl.

'And of course, as I was telling you, Mother, it's impossible for me to afford the trip on the little money that I have and yet it is the chance of a lifetime.'

'No soup for me, thank you, dear.' Mrs Leamington turned her attention back to her son. There was a worried look on her wrinkled old face. 'Do you really feel that you should go on this trip, Arthur?'

'Of course, I should go. But I can't unless you give me the money.' He sounded surly and impatient.

'But, dearest, I did explain to you . . .'

It was amazing that they would talk like that in front of her, thought Sarah, standing stiffly by the soup tureen. There was enough soup there to feed an orphanage and it smelt delicious, but it did not seem as if much was going to be consumed. Mrs Leamington was nervously crumbling a bread roll on her plate and her son had thrown down his spoon after swallowing a couple of mouthfuls.

'Take it away,' he barked at Sarah after a minute.

Silently Sarah removed the soup plates, placing both on the silver tray next to the heavy soup tureen. She prayed that she could hold the tray steadily in one hand while opening the door with her other, and smiled to herself as she managed to close the door behind her without spilling anything.

'Here's the next course ready for you, dear,' said Mrs Bailey when she came back into the kitchen. 'There, everything is on the tray. Ellen, you go and open the door for her.'

Ellen pushed open the door with a wink at Sarah, but once Sarah was safely in the dining room, it closed behind her with a bang. A gust of smoke whirled out from the chimney and circled through the room.

'Wine, sir?' murmured Sarah, trying to copy the refined tones that parlour maids always affected.

'Oh dear, this smoke!' said Mrs Leamington. 'I'm sorry about this, Arthur. We only had the sweep in the other day. I think we'll have to get him back again.'

'Why waste your money?' Arthur Leamington nodded to Sarah to fill his glass. 'I can't see any problem. It was just that servant of yours, letting the door bang. Why do you have to have such untrained servants? Come on, girl, fill it up!' He swallowed the whole contents of the glass and held it out for Sarah to refill.

Sarah poured the wine, trying to keep her expression blank.

'I mean it, Mother.' His tone was loud and bullying. 'You definitely need to think of the many ways in which you waste money and then are left with nothing on hand when there is an emergency.'

What an unpleasant bully that man is, thought Sarah, feeling sorry for the poor old woman. And why was he so reluctant to get Grimston back to the house again? Was there some connection between himself and that villainous master chimney sweep?

She looked at the large hand that was squeezing the stem of the wine glass as though he wanted to snap it in two. A powerful hand . . . a hand that could squeeze the throat of a frail boy. Could Arthur Leamington have choked the life out of Joe?

CHAPTER 12

STRANGE AND MAD

'Mr Leamington was so nasty! He came into the kitchen after dinner and asked all sorts of questions about me.' Sarah moved a little closer to the coal fire in the cellar. 'I can't stop shivering,' she said, putting her arm around Mutsy who was looking at her anxiously. 'It's just the way that man looked at me, as if he was mad with fury or something. He was shouting at the top of his voice at the poor cook.'

'What was he saying?' asked Alfie, sounding worried. How on earth could Arthur Leamington have suspected Sarah?

'He was yelling at her for taking in a girl off the

streets to wait at table. He was saying that I could rob or murder an old lady like his mother and he told her to get that beggar's brat out of the house immediately. Then he grabbed his hat and cloak and went off, slamming the door behind him.'

'Sounds like he was more bothered about you for his own sake than for his mother's – otherwise why leave then, why not wait until you was thrown out?' said Sammy shrewdly.

'You're right.' Sarah nodded. 'Perhaps he saw me looking at him when I was handing the vegetables to him and he read my mind. I was thinking that he and Grimston might both be in on the murder. That perhaps he saw Grimston strangle Joe. And then Grimston paid him something to keep quiet and to take the body away in his gig. Anyway,' she said, a bit more cheerfully, 'the missus was very nice. She told me to take no notice, that her son had business worries and that he wasn't himself and then she told the cook to give me the leftovers from the meal because I looked very thin and pale. The cook wrapped up the duck and the roasted potatoes and the lemon cake that they didn't even touch. She was just going to throw the soup down the sink when I asked if I could have that too. She put it in the milk can and then put all the bread rolls in a bag as well. I could hardly carry all the stuff by the time that I got out of the house.'

'I'd like some of that soup,' said Tom, opening the can and sniffing deeply. 'Smells of beef.'

'Not the soup,' said Alfie. Though he spoke slowly, his brain was working fast. 'Let's have the duck and the potatoes first and then the cake. Don't touch the soup or the bread rolls though; I've plans for those.'

'What . . .' began Tom, but his brother frowned at him. Jack understood that Alfie didn't want to be questioned just now.

'Do you think that Mr Leamington had anything to do with the murder of Joe?' asked Jack.

'I don't know,' Sarah said, biting into a succulent slice of duck – how could anyone leave meat like that on their plate? she wondered – 'but it's the only reason that I can think of for him getting so furious about me. He saw me looking at him and he knew that he had never seen me in his mother's house before and he got suspicious and asked Mrs Bailey about me.'

'Why should he think you were after him, though? You don't look like none of them peelers. Not very like, at least . . .' Tom laughed at his own wit and tossed a roasted potato to Mutsy who caught it neatly and swallowed it in one gulp.

'That's true,' said Sarah, 'but I suppose if you feel guilty, anything different worries you. I can't see any other reason for him to fly into such a temper.'

'Perhaps he thought his mother was spending money on a new servant instead of giving it to him,' pointed out Jack. 'You said that he was trying to get money from her and she was telling him that she couldn't afford it. He was trying to stop her getting the sweep again, wasn't he?'

'Yes, but if he had anything to do with Joe's death, then he wouldn't want Grimston coming back to the house again, would he?' argued Sarah. 'Perhaps it wasn't Grimston that murdered Joe, perhaps it was Mr Leamington – it could be that he was scared that Grimston might have seen something. Perhaps Joe saw him take money from his mother's purse and that's why Joe was murdered.'

'Sounds daft to me,' said Tom. 'Why strangle a sweeping boy for something like that? Joe wouldn't have dared to say a word to anyone.'

'You don't know what he's like,' said Sarah with a shudder. 'I'd say that murder would come easy to him. He has a strange, mad look in his eyes. I thought he was going to strangle me for a minute.' She got to her feet, feeling her legs tremble beneath her, and cut off half of the cake, putting it in the tin box above the fireplace. That will do the boys for their breakfast, she thought, trying to distract herself.

'You all right, Sarah?' asked Jack, looking at her with concern.

'I'm fine,' said Sarah resolutely. 'In fact, I quite enjoyed the waiting at table. I'm sure that I could do well as a parlour maid. I was thinking that I might look for a job at an inn as a parlour maid and then when I've had some experience I could go back into service again. What are you thinking about, Alfie?'

He had been very quiet while they ate, but suddenly he got to his feet. 'Jack and Tom, you take Sarah home. Me and Sammy are going back to Devil's Acre.'

'Back to Devil's Acre,' echoed Jack. 'Is that safe?'

'Here,' said Tom sharply, 'why are you taking that bag of bread rolls and the soup?'

'Feeding the hungry,' said Alfie briefly. He tipped the soup from the can into the blackened pot that hung on chains above the fire, watched it until it began to bubble, then poured it back into the can again, wrapping a ragged towel around the can to keep it warm.

Jack carefully banked down the fire with some wet

coal dust and waited, looking enquiringly at Alfie. Sammy stood up, stretched out an arm until he found Mutsy's warm bulk and then he grabbed the knotted piece of rope around the dog's neck.

'Come on, Sam,' said Alfie, placing the wrapped can of hot soup at the bottom of the bag given to Sarah by the cook and piling the bread rolls around it.

Jack looked at them both uneasily. Sarah watched him hesitate and then make up his mind to speak. 'Be careful, Alfie,' he said. 'If Grimston killed Joe . . . well, Joe may not have been the first . . .' He stopped and then continued slowly '. . . and he may not be Grimston's last murder.'

CHAPTER 13

HELL ON EARTH

Jack, Tom and Sarah walked briskly up St Martin's Lane and then turned up Monmouth Street, going towards Seven Dials. It was getting late, but the streets were full of people. St Martin's Lane was busy with well-dressed crowds going to the theatres or to restaurants, but in Monmouth Street there were more poor people than rich – mainly the poor who made a living from the rich, by begging, shoe-shining and stealing.

Jack, Tom and Sarah watched with indifference as three bare-footed boys followed a well-dressed gentleman. From time to time he looked over his shoulder in an uneasy way but, each time he did so, the three boys melted into the shadows of a doorway. They waited until the man reached a darker part of the street where a gas lamp had been extinguished, then they moved in quickly. One jostled him roughly, then apologised profusely, while the other two carefully held up his coat-tails and took a purse from one pocket and a fine linen handkerchief from the other. Then they were off, running fast towards St Giles. Sarah half smiled. It was so quickly and cleverly done, the gentleman had not even noticed that he had been robbed.

Seven Dials was roaring when they reached it. Bright lights from gas lamps and torches burned through the yellow fog, and charcoal fires flamed from iron baskets and braziers. There was noise everywhere: shrieks, screams, laughs, the crash of breaking glass, the thunder of beer casks rolling into cellars. At the end of each of the seven streets, which came together here like the spokes on a wheel, there was a public house and every public house was full of people drinking pints of cheap gin, howling and laughing and fighting and overflowing out onto the street.

'This place is like hell on earth!' shouted a man flying from the crowds. His hat was grabbed by one of his pursuers. Already his fancy coat had been snatched from him, his trousers were torn and lace from his shirt had been ripped off. One side of his face was bleeding and one eye was swelling up and already beginning to close from the bruise.

'Good business going on here tonight,' said a man in a cloth cap with a casual air. He looked closely at Jack. 'Seen you down by the river, collecting coal, ain't that right? Mug's game, that is! You should get into my way of business. I could use a strong lad like you. I've got my own boat, but you need two people – one to row and one to pull the bodies on board. Give you ten pence for every sovereign that I make from the stiffs. There's many of them have ten pounds in their pockets and then there's the false teeth – I can always get a good price for them at the markets.'

'No thanks,' said Jack awkwardly. 'I'd be no good at it. No offence,' he added. The idea of spending his days pulling dead bodies from the Thames turned his stomach, but it was better not to make enemies.

'None taken,' said the man grandly. He seemed very drunk and swayed as he spoke. 'I'd get out of here soon if I were you – get that little girl away. The cracksmen are in town tonight and things could get a bit rough. They're celebrating. Did a nice lot of jobs in the last few days. Cleared out a dozen houses, I heard . . .'

Jack followed his gaze towards a crowd of flashily dressed men and women outside one of the public houses – they must be the burglars the man was talking about.

And then suddenly everything changed. There was a clatter of horse hoofs on the paved surface of Monmouth Street. Another clatter from Queen Street, one from St Martin's Lane. Three cabs filled with policemen swept onto the square. A shot was fired in the air. Everyone scattered, screaming, and the cracksmen and their women friends moved hastily, some running into the public houses, others hurling glasses and tankards into the faces of the police. One pulled out a pistol and fired back at the police, and a man and woman raced towards a gig tied to a lamppost.

'Let's get out of here!' Jack seized Sarah by the arm and began to run.

Tom ran ahead and the other two followed him as fast as they could. There was another shot from behind them. Sarah turned to look over her shoulder and to her horror she saw the cracksman's gig coming after them, the woman wrapped in a shawl which went right across her face, the man, who wore a mask, cracking the whip, and the horse racing as fast as it could go.

'Get in to the side, Tom!' screamed Sarah. Jack was already heading towards a shop door, but at that instant, a button broke from Sarah's shoe. She wobbled unsteadily, her ankle was wrenched. She looked back over her shoulder again quickly. The shawl had fallen from the woman's face and Sarah shrieked, 'Mavis!'

For a moment, she thought that the parlour maid had been abducted by the thief, but then Mavis looked straight at Sarah and screamed, 'Run her down, Arthur! She's seen me!'

And the cracksman drove his gig straight at Sarah.

CHAPTER 14

DEVIL'S ACRE

The fog was dense as Alfie, Sammy and Mutsy walked down towards Westminster. They walked side by side, Sammy holding tightly to the knotted rope, Mutsy carefully steering him past obstacles and around people, and Alfie stumbling and peering as the fog grew thicker. Eventually he gave up trying to see and took his brother's arm; they would just have to trust to Mutsy to lead them safely.

'Should have left you at home, Sam,' he said eventually. 'Didn't realise that the fog was this thick.'

'Don't make no difference to me,' said Sammy with a chuckle and Mutsy wagged his tail. Alfie could feel it beating against his bare ankles like a wet rope.

'In any case,' went on Sammy, 'you probably have an idea in your head. Never knowed you when you didn't have an idea, Alfie.'

Alfie smiled in the dark mist. Sammy could always read his mind. 'That's right,' he admitted. 'I just thought these fellows, these chimney sweeping boys, might be willing to talk to you a bit. People sometimes do and these fellows are like scared rabbits.'

'Maybe, maybe not,' said Sammy thoughtfully. 'People are mostly sorry for me and that's why they don't mind chatting to me. These boys will only be sorry for themselves. I'm better off than them. Where are we now, Alfie?'

'Blessed if I know.' Alfie screwed up his eyes tightly and peered through the fog. He could only see a few yards ahead of him. The one good thing was that there didn't seem to be any traffic on the road – no sound of horse hoofs, no wheel noises from cabs, gigs, carts or carriages. He half wondered whether to give up and try to find the way home, but the heavy bag in his hand reminded him of the good opportunity that he had of getting those half-starved boys to talk – and they knew something, he was sure of that.

'It might be better to go along beside the river,' he

said. 'There's usually some boats with lights on at night and they'll light up the water a bit.'

'Easy enough to find the river,' said Sammy cheerfully. 'Go on, Mutsy, river! Use your nose, boy. Smells extra bad tonight, don't it?'

Alfie sniffed. The fog did make the smell worse – it would be nice to get a wind, he thought, but at least it wasn't freezing. He wasn't wearing the boots; he had decided that they had to be kept for special occasions. In any case, they were not very comfortable as he had bought them far too big so that they could also fit Jack if he ever needed to look smart.

Alfie was right: the river was quite visible. The pitch torches burning alongside it gave more light than the gas lamps and their red glow was reflected in the water. He let go of Sammy's arm and stuck a hand into the bag and touched the can of soup. There was a faint warmth coming from it and the bread smelt appetising.

'There's the abbey ahead. Bit clearer now, too,' he said with relief. 'I can see the windows lit up.' He had been dreading coming to this place in the fog, as the area all around Westminster Abbey was marshy. 'This way, Mutsy!'

'What are you doing?' asked Sammy.

'Just borrowing a torch,' said Alfie. 'All right for you: you can listen to the boys. I want to see them.' It was an offence to remove one of the pitch torches, but he hoped that no policeman would want to wander around Devil's Acre in the dark.

The Mitre & Dove public house was doing good business and the light spilt out across the pavement in front of it and from the kitchen into the yard behind. Alfie skirted it carefully, keeping in the shadow of the old crumbling wall.

'We'll feed them first and then ask the questions,' he murmured to Sammy as he steered his brother away from the large pool of stagnant water.

There was no sound from the stable when they approached it. Alfie went ahead, holding the torch high, and stopped at the crumbling doorway. No wood was left, but someone had hung a filthy sack up to keep out the worst of the rain. Alfie pushed it aside and peered in.

'Come on, boy, in you go,' he said encouragingly to Mutsy. He removed Sammy's hand from the knotted piece of rope. He didn't fancy going into the place until Mutsy checked it for rats, so he stayed at the doorway with Sammy, pointing the pitch torch in to light up every detail of crumbling, rotten plaster, leaking roof, putrid growths of fungi, and piles of filth where the boys had not bothered going outside to relieve themselves.

Sure enough, Mutsy pounced and the next moment a large rat that was just about to scuttle away met its death with a loud squeal. The boys sat up hurriedly, the youngest one bleeding from where the rat had just bitten him on the arm. He began to cry hopelessly and Alfie quickly opened his bag and shoved a bun into the boy's hand. For a moment it almost seemed as though he was too dazed to know what to do, but then he crammed it into his mouth and stared at Mutsy who was munching the rat noisily.

'Plenty for everyone.' Alfie decided to give out the buns first to relax them all, then he could share out the soup. He opened the can and even in that stinking stable the delicious smell of beef soup rose up.

But that was a mistake.

The three boys were not the only hungry creatures in Devil's Acre.

CHAPTER 15

MURDER
IS EASY

The horse reared up just beside Sarah. For one terror-filled moment, she could see the horse's wild eyes and its red nostrils, hear its panting, feel its hot breath on her neck, the iron-shod hoofs glinting within a few inches of her head.

It would crush her skull, she thought. She had seen something like that once, where a child at St Giles had escaped from her gin-sodden mother and had run beneath the feet of a horse.

For a second she was paralysed by the thought; then she dropped to the ground, crouching with her knees at her chest, her arms around her head.

A stunning blow hit her on the back of her ribs. The pain was so bad that she felt as if she would die. She couldn't breathe. Her muscles cramped. Sweat ran down her forehead, into her eyes and down her cheeks. A sudden feeling of heat swept over her; then she was icy cold and shivering, teeth chattering, odd ripples and trembles going up her back.

And then she heard a familiar voice. 'Whoa, boy, whoa, easy now, boy, good boy.' It was Jack, soothing, praising, coaxing, talking to the horse, calming him down.

And then another voice, harsh, belligerent, full of fury with a note of fear in it. 'Get out of my way! Don't you touch my horse! Let him go or I'll kill you! Take that and clear off.'

'Jack!' screamed Tom's voice.

Then the gig went right over her head, the nearside wheel rolling right in front of her arms, miraculously missing her by less than an inch.

Sarah stayed very still. Jack bent over her and she screamed when he lifted her awkwardly under the arms. She sat up, pushing her hair out of her eyes and looking down at her black dress. It was covered in mud and for a moment that mattered more than the pain in her ribs. She tried to get up, but the pain flared again and she sank back gasping.

'Just hold my elbows, the two of you,' she said through gritted teeth.

They helped her up and to her amazement Sarah found that she could walk. The terrible pain was becoming bearable, though she still gasped and sweated. When she reached the doorway of a shop, she leant against it, closing her eyes. She was still alive, and not crushed beneath the horse's hoofs, or sliced in two by the wheel of the gig.

Tom was saying, 'My God, Sarah, I thought you were a goner. That horse was within an inch of trampling you when Jack grabbed him.'

Sarah looked at Jack. By the light of the gas lamp overhead, she could see that his face was slashed from eye to chin. It was bleeding, but Jack was grinning.

'Bad-tempered fella like that shouldn't be allowed to own a nice horse.'

Sarah laughed shakily. 'All horses are nice to you, Jack.' He had saved her life, but she knew him well enough to understand that it would embarrass him terribly to be thanked. She took a clean handkerchief from her pocket and handed it to him. 'Keep that over your cheek for now, then wash that cut as soon as you can – and make sure that you boil the water first. I'll get some salve from the cook and bring it along tomorrow night.'

'Why did that fellow want to run you down, Sarah?' asked Tom.

Sarah shivered. 'It wasn't him, it was Mavis. The parlour maid from Number Four Goodwin's Court. I saw her with the cracksman and I called out her name, then she told him to run me down.' But what was it that Mavis had called the cracksman? Arthur, that's what she had said. It couldn't be Mr Leamington – or could it? The voice had seemed different, rougher, but then it could have been faked and in any case the mask over his face would have muffled the sound.

'But why? You could have been killed!' said Jack.

Sarah was quiet for a moment, remembering the moment when her eyes met Mavis's. 'I was a fool to call her name out. No one would want a servant of theirs to be associated with burglars. And a parlour maid is a very responsible position. A parlour maid gets paid more than double what a scullery maid like me gets. She knew she'd lose her job if I told anyone. The easiest thing would be to get rid of me – and she nearly did.' She shuddered a little. 'Murder is easy; getting a new job is much harder.'

Both Jack and Tom nodded. They knew how hard

it was to get by without a job.

'She was afraid you'd carry tales to her mistress and then she'd be out of work,' Tom summed up. His eyes widened suddenly. 'But do you think Mavis murdered Joe too?'

'I don't know,' said Sarah thoughtfully. 'It changes everything if we know that she is going out with a cracksman. Perhaps she had sneaked him into the kitchen and Joe came unexpectedly back down there and saw her with him.'

Jack said nothing, pressed the handkerchief into his wounded cheek.

'Or maybe the cracksman had done a job at Goodwin's Court!' said Tom excitedly. 'Maybe Joe saw a burglary.'

'Could be,' said Jack, looking from one face to the other. 'That's an idea, Tom.'

'No.' Sarah tried to laugh, but almost burst into tears instead. 'It doesn't make sense. We'd have heard if anything was stolen from Number Four. The cook would have mentioned it. I'm sure it was because Mavis thought I would carry tales about her. They just needed to keep me quiet – even if it meant killing me.' She swallowed hard and managed to regain her composure. 'Now, let's get on, for goodness' sake. I'll have to be up half the night if I am going to get this gown fit to wear for the morning – and I have to sew that button back onto my shoe.'

What will Alfie say about this? wondered Sarah as they walked along in silence. Perhaps Tom had a point. After all there were other houses in Goodwin's Court – all of them owned by rich people probably. She tried to think about it, but then gave up. She felt too shaky and ill for thinking logically. Her ribs were still very sore, but she was relieved to be able to walk. If her leg had been kicked by the horse, then she would have been unable to work – her job as a scullery maid meant that she was continually scurrying in and out of the kitchen, the sculleries, the pantries and the yard. She was lucky really, she thought, as they turned into Bloomsbury Square and paused outside the big house where she lived and worked. Her ribs might be cracked but she could put up with pain.

'We'll wait until you get in,' said Jack.

Sarah nodded, went down the little side alleyway, found her key, inserted it into the keyhole, turned to wave at Jack and Tom, and then froze.

A familiar gig had come slowly along the side of Bloomsbury Square. There was just one person in it now, just a man. He was keeping his horse at a slow walk, scanning the pavements, obviously looking for someone. As she looked, his eyes met hers and lingered there. Then she saw him look at the front door of the house, as if he were memorising the number.

It was the man with the mask on his face, the man that Mavis called Arthur, the man who had tried to murder her half an hour ago. He would know her name already: now he knew where she lived.

But who was this Arthur?

CHAPTER 16

A Swarm
of Rats

All had been going well at Devil's Acre. They all sat around in a ring. Alfie managed to find a stone for himself and Sammy and the three sweeping boys sat on the heap of straw. Each boy had gulped down his share of the heavenly smelling meat soup, each had stuffed bun after bun into their mouths.

Alfie waited. He still had three buns left in his bag. He'd made no secret of that, peering into the bag by the light of the torch and counting aloud. They knew there would be more to come.

'What's your names?' he asked casually. Always start with the easy questions, he told himself.

'I'm Frank and the little fella is Bert, my brother,' said the oldest boy.

'And I'm Bill,' said the middle boy, his eyes fixed longingly on the bag.

'Why did old Grimston strangle Joe?' asked Alfie. He shot the words out quickly.

'Did he?' asked Bill, while, almost at the same second, Frank said, 'So that's what happened to Joe.'

'You don't sound surprised – not the first time, was it, that Grimston strangled a boy?' Alfie kept his voice confident and assured.

'So you know about Isaac, do you?' said Frank after a moment's pause.

And then Bert screamed. Screamed and pointed.

Above their heads was a hole in the roof. And through that hole a long, sinuous shadow seemed to be flowing, like water from a jug. Alfie lifted the torch, shone it on the moving mass and then jumped to his feet with a cry of alarm.

'Let's get out of here!' he shouted, grabbing Sammy by the arm and hauling him to his feet. The other boys followed hard on their heels.

Hundreds of rats were pouring down in a long stream of small heads, humped backs and bare tails. Mutsy barked once and then attacked, but there were too many rats even for him. They ran from his lethal, jaws, but they followed the boys outside, snapping at the food in little Bert's hand. Bert shrieked again and Alfie felt claws run across his bare feet. He swirled the pitch torch, driving it into the swarm. There was a high-pitched squeal, a smell of burning, and the rats retreated from the fire.

Bert sobbed, Frank swore and picked up a broken piece of wood, flailing it around. Alfie seized another piece of wood from under the eaves of the stable and held the torch to it. The worm-eaten timber kindled instantly, sending up an orange flame, as Alfie dropped it to the ground to create a flaming barrier.

'More wood!' screamed Alfie. 'Get some more wood, you three!' He dared not move. He had to keep next to Sammy. Mutsy was fighting a hard battle against the rats. They had learnt that his teeth were deadly but they ran behind him and now Mutsy was wasting energy, whirling around, trying to kill as many as he could.

Then Frank put some more wood on Alfie's fire. It blazed up, revealing a scene of horror. Rats were everywhere, climbing down walls, running across the cobbled yard, swimming through the stagnant pool of sewage. For the moment, the dog and the fire were protecting the five boys, but that was not going to last. Sooner rather than later, one rat, bolder than the others, would brave that swinging torch, would rush past those snapping jaws and where one rat went, then the rest would follow . . .

Alfie made up his mind. 'Mutsy, here boy,' he said and obediently Mutsy joined him. Alfie transferred Sammy's hand to the knotted rope on Mutsy's collar.

'Go home, boy, take Sammy home,' he said. There was no time to waste on explanations.

Quickly Alfie took one of the buns from his bag. Handing the torch to Frank, he broke the bun into ten pieces and tossed them at the rats. Instantly they all turned towards the food, an appalling horde of screaming, scrabbling, squirming and biting as they fought for the pieces of bread.

Alfie took the torch back from Frank. By now Sammy and Mutsy had gone through the gate, Mutsy towing Sammy along at such speed that the blind boy was running. The clever dog had understood that he had to get Sammy away from the menace of the rats.

Alfie made himself wait until they were out on the street. Now he knew what he should do. It would take a steady nerve and a lot of luck. Once through the gate, he would be almost at the back yard of the

Mitre & Dove public house. And outside that yard stood ten tall dustbins.

Alfie fumbled with his left hand in the bag and drew out the second bun. Now he suddenly began to run, crumbling the bun as he went.

The rats came after him – there were so many of them that he could hear the patter of their naked claws on the cobblestoned surface.

As he ran, Alfie dropped pieces of bun behind him. If only there was enough to last!

He was fast through the gate, but the rats were at his heels. He half turned, swung the torch in a semi-circle behind him and dropped the last piece of the second bun. It was a fairly big piece and once again the rats fought over it.

Now Alfie had reached the dustbins. The lid of each one was weighed down by a large stone. Quickly he tipped the nearest stone to the ground, risking placing his precious, flaming torch on top of it. The torch was dying down; the flame had almost consumed the tar. Soon it would be useless to him, but for the moment it was the only thing that stood between him and the rats.

Then Alfie lifted the dustbin lid and stood with it in his right hand. His left hand drew out the last bun.

Alfie took a deep breath. He held up the broken bun. Two hundred small, glittering eyes looked up at him. Quickly Alfie threw the bread into the tall bin. Already it was half full of putrid scraps of waste food. The rats did not hesitate. They swarmed up the side of the bin and dropped down on the food. Soon they were piled up almost to the top. There was just enough room.

Alfie clanged the lid down and quickly added the stone. Then took another stone and another until the lid was weighted down. He picked up his torch. His legs were trembling but he waved a cheerful salute towards the boys and then turned to go out onto the street.

At that very moment, a cart swung in from Westminster. A man swore, a whip was flung around Alfie's neck, half-strangling him and causing him to drop the torch as he clawed desperately at the choking leather.

'So it's you,' said a voice.

It was Grimston, the master chimney sweep.

CHAPTER 17

MURDEROUS EYES

Alfie stood very still. He could not fight that strangle-hold. The door of the public house opened and two men came out, laughing loudly and clutching at each other, hardly able to stand. Alfie saw at a glance that they were both very drunk, but even so he tried to attract their attention by coughing wildly.

The men took little notice, but Grimston loosened his whip and Alfie managed to get a hand between his neck and the leather.

'Good evening, Mr Grimston,' he croaked.

'What are you doing here?' hissed Grimston. He looked back towards the stables. The three boys stood beside the fire and their shadows reared up black against the stone wall. They seemed to be frozen with fear.

'Get back into your kennel or I'll whip you to death,' shouted Grimston, cracking his horsewhip loudly. 'Who lit that fire?' he yelled.

None of the boys answered. They melted away, their shadows getting smaller, and then they were gone behind the piece of sacking over the doorway.

'I lit it,' said Alfie. By now he had managed to free his neck of the whip. He picked up the torch. Miraculously it was still alight. He felt safer with it – almost brave as he faced the master chimney sweep.

The noise was very loud from the public house – shouts, laughs, the sad wail of a fiddle, snatches of song – but there was another noise underneath it . . . an insistent drumming sound and Alfie knew what it was. The rats were trying to get out of the metal rubbish bin.

He faced up to Grimston. 'I lit that fire,' he repeated. The fragile body of the little fellow, Bert, was in his mind. If Grimston whipped him with that horsewhip, he would probably kill the child.

'Oh, you did, did you?' Grimston advanced upon Alfie and gave the whip one more suggestive crack.

'Yes, I did,' said Alfie. 'I came to give you a message. It's a message from my father,' he lied. In his mind he focused on this imaginary father. A big, stout man, bigger than Grimston. Prosperous, too. Some sort of business. A carter, that was it. Brought fruit and vegetables into Covent Garden every day. Sold them for a good price. A man with money, with influence . . .

'What were you meddling with my boys for?'

'Just brought them a few things to eat – they looked hungry.' Alfie edged a little nearer to the public house yard.

'What do you mean they looked hungry? What business of yours is it?' Grimston followed him, still with the whip swinging from his hand. Alfie wished that he had worn his boots. They gave him a feeling of superiority and they would be useful for kicking.

'Go on, then, answer the question,' roared Grimston.

The door of the public house opened again. This time the three men who came out seemed a little less drunk. They stared curiously at Grimston and then at Alfie.

Alfie moved a little nearer to the yard. 'I'm afraid I have to go now, Mr Grimston,' he said politely. 'My father is waiting for me around the corner, over there.' He pointed and Grimston followed the direction of the finger. It was almost impossible to see anything. There was just a glow of light from Westminster Abbey, a few misty gas lamps and the lit-up windows of the Mitre & Dove.

Alfie moved again while the man's eye was off him. Now he could almost touch the wall of the yard.

Grimston turned back to face him. By the light of the torch his face looked uncertain.

'He asked me to tell you that he has changed his mind about sending my little stepbrother to you,' said Alfie politely.

'Oh, he has, has he?' Now Grimston sounded belligerent, but he glanced over his shoulder in an uneasy way.

I shouldn't do this, thought Alfie. I'm crazy. Why not get away now while he's a bit unsure, while these three men are still within earshot? But he knew what he was going to do before the words left his mouth.

'You see, he has heard all about . . .' Alfie paused to give his next word emphasis. '. . . Isaac!'

At that name, Grimston roared like a bull. He rushed at Alfie, his powerful hands ready to clamp around the boy's throat.

Alfie coolly flipped the iron lid from the nearest

dustbin, neatly avoiding the stones that crashed to the ground.

A hundred rats flowed over the edge, down the side, avoided Alfie's blazing pitch torch and headed straight towards Grimston.

CHAPTER 18

MISSING BOY

'It was the funniest thing you've ever seen.' Alfie rested his feet on the chimney breast and took a bite from the last slice of lemon cake. He was in a mood to celebrate.

'Did he screech, with all the rats running around his legs?' asked Tom eagerly.

'Near split the walls with the noise he was making,' said Alfie with enormous satisfaction. 'The horse went wild too – started running around the yard and the cart behind it was crashing and banging and the rats were running up the horse's legs to avoid the kicks, and then all the people from the public house came rushing out and they had sticks and they was hitting at the rats and then one of them cracksmen came out with a pistol and started firing shots everywhere. A miracle no one was killed.'

Alfie took another bite of the sweet lemon cake. Actually, he had not seen too much of the excitement – though he had heard the noise. He had quietly slid away down towards the Thames, where he had replaced the torch into its holder and then made his way home.

'I like the bit where you took the lid off the rubbish bin,' said Tom, still chuckling. 'Wish I had been there.'

'So he went mad when you mentioned the name Isaac. That's interesting.' Sammy chewed thoughtfully.

'Who's Isaac, anyway?' asked Jack. He came forward and added some more coal to the fire – this was a night to enjoy. He could easily get more coal tomorrow morning, he reasoned.

'Jeepers, what happened to your face, Jack?' Alfie stared at the slash on his cousin's cheek.

'Tell you about that in a minute.' As usual, Jack didn't want to talk about himself. 'Go on, who is this Isaac?'

'It was when we was talking to the three sweeping boys,' explained Sammy. 'Alfie asked them why old Grimston strangled Joe. He asked them quick like, so that they had no time to think about it.'

'And Bill, he's one of the boys, said "Did he?"' continued Alfie, 'and then Frank said, "So that's what happened to Joe".'

'And Alfie just said, cool as a breeze, "You don't sound surprised – not the first time, was it, that Grimston strangled a boy".' Sammy was a good mimic.

'And that,' said Alfie dramatically, 'was when Frank, the eldest fellow, said, "So you know about Isaac, do you?"' He turned to Sammy. 'How do you think that he sounded when he said that, Sam?'

'Scared,' said Sammy without a moment's hesitation. 'And he was surprised – but mostly he was just frightened.'

'So Grimston has already killed a boy, is that what you're thinking, Alfie?' asked Jack.

'I'd say so,' said Alfie with conviction.

'But what would that have to do with Joe?' Tom sounded puzzled.

'If he killed one boy, he would kill another boy,' said Sammy quietly. 'I'd say that murder is one of those things that the oftener you do it, the easier it is to do.'

'I might have a word with Inspector Denham tomorrow,' said Alfie. 'He'd know if Grimston was ever accused of murdering a boy called Isaac. Didn't mention it, though. He must have got off or else he'd have been hanged by now.'

'Maybe no one found the body,' said Jack. 'If Grimston, or whoever it was, had thrown Joe's body a couple of feet further, it would have gone straight into the river and got washed to shore a mile or two downstream. Joe would probably have ended up at London Bridge or perhaps even further. Maybe that's what happened to this Isaac.'

Alfie nodded. It was only because he had found Joe and had recognised him that Grimston was now under suspicion. Did Grimston know, he wondered, that he was the one who found the body? He shivered when he thought of that; there was no doubt that the man would not hesitate to murder him if he found out that Alfie was working with Inspector Denham.

'But you're forgetting about the gig.' Sammy's voice broke into his thoughts. 'Joe was flung out of a gig, not a cart.'

'Perhaps Grimston could have stolen the gig – taken it from one of the yards behind the houses in Goodwin's Court,' said Alfie. 'Mrs Leamington's son, Arthur, leaves his gig in her yard when he comes to visit. Where does he live anyway, I wonder – the son,

I mean. That's another thing to find out when I go to Goodwin's Court tomorrow morning to look at the chimney.'

He gave an enormous yawn. 'I'm off to bed now,' he said. 'I've asked the night watchman to bang on the window tomorrow at six o'clock. But tell us about your cheek before I go to sleep, Jack.'

'That parlour maid from Goodwin's Court was out with her fancy man,' said Tom eagerly. 'One of the swells, one of the cracksmen from Seven Dials, it was. Sarah sees her and she's so shocked she sings out at the top of her voice "Mavis!" and this Mavis yells, "Run her down, Arthur!" and the swell geezer does just that. He drives his gig right at Sarah. He pulls the horse up on its back legs and there it was, rearing over Sarah. She got kicked, but just in the ribs. Jack saved her. He grabbed the reins and quietened the horse down and —'

'Is Sarah all right?' asked Sammy.

'She said she was,' said Jack. 'Ribs will be sore for a few days, though, I'd say.'

'Arthur?' questioned Alfie, looking from one to the other. 'It were never Arthur Leamington, were it?'

Jack shrugged his shoulders. 'Don't know,' he said briefly. 'Sarah don't know either. The fella had a mask on, covered most of his face, and his cloak was pulled up around the chin.'

'Can't imagine a toff like him to be going out with a parlour maid – even if she is so stuck-up,' said Alfie doubtfully. 'And taking her down Seven Dials. Not his sort of place at all.'

'Tried to murder Sarah, though,' put in Tom.

'Good job you was there, Jack,' said Alfie. 'Well, I'm off to sleep now.'

'But wait, Alfie,' Tom said in a hurry, 'that parlour maid, she might be mixed up with Joe's murder, mightn't she? And that Arthur Leamington.'

'What's they got to do with Joe?' asked Alfie, doubtfully.

'Well, she lives in the house where he was last seen alive What if the old lady's son is her fancy man and he did some burglaries down Goodwin's Court, and Joe spotted something? He and Mavis were ready enough to kill Sarah – they would have murdered Joe without blinking!'

'I don't know,' said Alfie. He didn't think it too likely that a man like Arthur Leamington would get mixed up with housemaids and cracksmen at Seven Dials, but Tom was easily offended if he thought his ideas were not taken seriously. 'Let's think about it in the morning,' he added with another yawn.

'You know what I think, Alfie,' said Sammy. 'I think that we all need to be careful. There's an awful lot of murderous people hanging around these days.'

CHAPTER 19

ALFIE
GETS A SHOCK

Ellen, the scullery maid, was still in her nightcap and wrapper when she opened the back door of Number Four Goodwin's Court to Alfie. She rubbed her eyes sleepily and then said, 'Where are your brushes?'

'Left them outside for the moment till I prepare everything,' said Alfie, whose quick wits rarely deserted him.

'Suit yourself,' said Ellen. 'I'm going back to get dressed. Be as quick as you can. The place will be freezing cold until we can light the fires. Missus isn't too happy about you coming, anyway. She said that we should have got Grimston back; it's his job to put the chimney right. He's been doing her chimneys for the last ten years, that's what she said. She's sent for him, but since you are here you might as well have a go. There's sixpence for you when you're finished.'

'Won't take long,' said Alfie cheerfully. He didn't like the sound of the master chimney sweep being summoned, but he was hopeful that he would be gone long before the man arrived. Mr Grimston would be sure to have other jobs lined up before he could get to Goodwin's Court.

'There's a lantern there for you on the table,' said Ellen. 'Make sure that you don't drop it. Any breakages will have to be paid for.'

'You can trust me. I know what I am doing,' said Alfie, eyeing the chimney breast in a professional manner. He was glad to see that only a few dead coals lay in the fireplace. 'You go back and get dressed and leave it all to me,' he said in a kindly fashion.

Alfie had little notion of how a chimney sweep set to work, but he knew he had to go up there and try to see what Joe had seen on that day.

Joe's words to him still rang in his head. Alfie went over the phrases again – by now he had them by heart: something about a bend . . . something about going the wrong way or into a wrong room . . . something about being scared . . .

Alfie wished now that he had taken more careful notice, had talked for longer to Joe, had held onto him until he understood what the boy was trying to say, but it was too late to change the past. All he could be sure of was that Joe had climbed this chimney in front of him, had emerged, terrified, on the roof, had gone to the extent of trying to escape – walking along the rooftops and climbing down to St Martin's Lane – but had he gone back nonetheless?

Alfie wondered whether to take off his coat and just keep on his shirt and trousers – he had seen what soot did to cloth. Then he decided to keep everything on. He had worn the worst of his few clothes, and they would help to protect his knees and elbows. Reluctantly he approached the chimney. He was too big for a chimney sweeping boy; he knew that. Grimston had said that even Joe was getting too big, and Alfie would make two of poor Joe, whose body had been skinny, with arms like sticks.

He stood peering up the chimney. There was a ledge a few feet up and he reckoned that he could put the lantern on that. Joe had done a good job on that last morning of his life. The chimney was well scraped, though the soot still clung to the rough edges of the stones and lodged in little nooks and crannies as far up as he could see.

'Here goes!' said Alfie aloud. He stuck his head and shoulders into the chimney and then gasped. He felt as though he was choking. The terrible acrid smell of soot filled his nose and mouth and stung his eyes. He shut his mouth and tried not to breathe, but his eyes poured with water and he could no longer see the ledge. He sank down onto his knees and pulled his head out of the chimney. He had never imagined that it could be as bad as that.

Once out, he shook the water from his eyes and looked around. There was a small rail over the kitchen sink with some spotless dishcloths hanging stiffly from it. Without hesitation he seized one, switched on the tap, soaked it, wrung it out and then fastened it securely over his nose and mouth.

And then once more he turned back. He could not give up yet.

This time he reached up and placed the lantern on the small shelf within the chimney before trying to climb. There was an almost new candle burning brightly inside the glass and he thought it would last well. It made the chimney seem less smothering to him.

Alfie edged his way up until he stood on the ledge beside the lantern. The wet cloth over his nose and mouth saved him from the worst of the soot and so far, he was thankful to find, there seemed to be room for his shoulders.

But he didn't know what to do next. Balancing precariously on the shelf, he held up the lantern. The chimney went on slanting upwards to the left but he couldn't see its end. How on earth did those small chimney sweeping boys go right up to the roof? This seemed to be the only ledge, as far as Alfie could see. He shone the light again, lighting up all four sides, but there were no more ledges, not even a protruding brick or stone to help him to lever himself up.

There was nothing for it but to use his bare feet, his elbows and his knees.

Leaving his lantern on the ledge, Alfie wriggled up the chimney. His feet were as hard as leather, but his elbows, even though covered with the shirt and coat, were soon scraped and bleeding. He ignored the pain. If he stopped he would lose courage, and he was determined to find out what had scared Joe. His breath came in sobs; the tightly tied dishcloth no longer helped, but at least his eyes were not streaming now. From time to time he glanced down. The light wasn't much help at this distance, but it gave him courage. He hated the inky, stifling blackness of the place. How could anyone do a job like this?

And then his groping hand met open space above. He made a tremendous effort, ignoring the pain of his scraped and bleeding knees and elbows, and tried to haul himself up into the opening. It didn't work – he started to slip down the chimney, but his feet saved him from going too far. He tried to take in a deep breath, but that just sucked the dishcloth into his mouth. He made one last attempt with his elbows, his feet scrabbling wildly for a grip, and then his chin rested on a platform. Cautiously he put one hand up, using his knees to hold his position, and then the second hand. Now he could pull himself up.

The kitchen chimney had led into the main chimney – he could see grey daylight far above him. He wished that he had the lamp, but he was getting better at seeing in the semi-darkness. It seemed as though he was standing at a crossroads. Two passageways led up from the groundfloor into the main chimney: one slanting up from the left and the other from the right – that was the one he had climbed up from the kitchen. That made sense, he thought, trying to think of the lay-out of the terraced house. In his mind's eye he could see the chimney coming out on the tallest part of the roof slope. He guessed that the main chimney would be in the centre of the house. The kitchen was at the back, so the other passageway to the left of him probably led up from the dining room – Sarah had said that was at the front of the house.

But in the opposite corners of the square main chimney, there were two more passages, one also going to the left, and one to the right. Alfie frowned. Where did they go? Surely there were only two rooms on the ground floor, he thought, but everything was confusing in this dark, airless place. The safest thing was to go straight up the main chimney and come out on the roof, so Alfie started to climb again – hands, elbows, toes, feet and knees all frantically scrabbling to grip and to raise him up, inch by inch.

After going up about another ten or fifteen feet, he came across another set of openings. Once more, he had a choice of five ways to go: he could carry on climbing upwards towards the roof, or he could go down one of the four sloping passageways. Alfie stopped for a moment and thought of Joe's words. What was it that he had said? A bend . . . going the wrong way. The right way would be to go straight up, or down the two passageways nearer to him. They were probably going to the fireplaces in the rooms above the dining room and the kitchen – must be the drawing room and Mrs Leamington's bedroom. Alfie made up his mind. He would go the *wrong* way.

Alfie chose the right-hand passageway furthest from him and stretched out a hand to test the ledge of the opening. This passage would be easier than the others, he decided, as it had a thick layer of soot on it.

Then his outstretched hand met something. There was a heap of something there in the openings – sticking out from the side chimney and half blocking the main chimney that went up to the roof. It was smooth and rounded, but it did not have the hard feel of stone, it was something brittle. Cautiously he felt around. Sticks, he thought, there's a whole lot of sticks here. Must be a rook's nest. His mouth stretched in a grin. He had found what was blocking the chimney – he was as good as any professional chimney sweep!

And yet these objects did not feel exactly like sticks, not even like sticks with the bark stripped off them. They were too smooth – smooth, but with little knobs on them here and there. Well, whatever they were, they needed to be removed. One by one, Alfie pushed them down the neck of his shirt. They felt cold against his bare skin. He went a little further down the side chimney and then his groping hand felt something else. This was bigger. It was rounded, smooth and very solid. Somehow he found room for it inside his shirt too.

The sticks were uncomfortable. Oddly enough, they didn't break but stayed there within his shirt, digging into his flesh. He had begun to guess what these objects might be, but he wouldn't be sure until he brought them into the light. Was this what had frightened Joe?

He climbed back down the main chimney slowly and carefully using his elbows and knees until he reached the lower landing. By now he was sick of wriggling so he stuck his legs into what he imagined must be the kitchen chimney sloping off the main chimney and slid the whole way down.

Alfie landed lightly on the coals, but his shirt caught on a protruding stone and the sticks fell out and scattered around the fireplace. His eyes were streaming and he had to mop them with the damp dishcloth before he could see anything. But then he caught his breath.

As he'd suspected, they weren't sticks. They were human bones. He put his hand inside his shirt, took out the rounded object and stared. It was a skull!

There was a piercing scream.

The old lady Mrs Leamington was standing by the table. The cook had her arm around her mistress, and Ellen was by the cupboard with her hands over her mouth.

And by the door stood Grimston.

CHAPTER 20

STRANGLING IS EASY

At the big house in Bloomsbury Square, Sarah struggled through her work in a mist of pain. It was lucky, she thought dully, that the horse had kicked her on the left side. Otherwise it would hardly have been possible for her to scrub dirty saucepans, scouring them with sand until her arm ached, or carry heavy buckets of filthy water to the sink hole in the yard. As it was, she could just about manage. She wished that she could get another job. She was sick of being a scullery maid. The work was so hard. She had enjoyed her few hours as a parlour maid at Goodwin's Court. It was a job that she knew she could do. But how could she get anyone to try her out as a parlour maid?

'What's the matter, love?' Mrs Miller, the cook at Bloomsbury Square, was a kindly woman. She stopped her work of kneading the dough for the day's bread baking and looked at Sarah with concern. 'You're as white as a sheet,' she said. 'Aren't you well?'

'I'm fine,' said Sarah, but she could not help the tears welling into her eyes.

'Here,' said the cook, 'sit down for a moment. You can tell me . . .'

Sarah sat down. The wish to tell her troubles was suddenly too much for her. It wasn't the pain – that would go. It was the thought that someone had tried to kill her that troubled her so much.

'I got kicked in the ribs by a horse,' she said, trying to smile.

'Is it bad?' The cook rushed to the oven, took out the first batch of breakfast rolls and thrust one into Sarah's hand, her eyes wide with sympathy.

'It's pretty black and blue,' said Sarah. The roll was still too hot to eat, but its heat was comforting. She tossed it mechanically from hand to hand to cool it and looked up at the cook.

She was a nice woman, Mrs Miller. She came from

the country and still spoke with a soft, country accent. She was always kind to Sarah and tried to protect her from the housekeeper, who was terribly strict with under-servants like the scullery maid and the knife boy.

'What happened? Did you slip and fall?' Mrs Miller had her back turned and was rooting on the shelf where she kept her salves for all sorts of illnesses and injuries.

'No . . .' Suddenly Sarah decided to tell the truth. She bit into the hot roll. It was delicious. Mrs Miller would listen kindly to what Sarah had to say, might even advise her about what to do. Perhaps it would all make sense when she went over it again. 'I think someone deliberately tried to kill me,' she said in a low voice.

Mrs Miller whirled around, salve in hand, and came back to the table. She sat down heavily. 'What?' she exclaimed. Her mouth fell open as Sarah began to tell her about what happened at Seven Dials. Her expression grew more and more horrified as she listened to the story.

'You should go to the police,' she said with conviction when Sarah had finished. 'I think it's your duty. That parlour maid shouldn't keep her position.'

'I'd hate to think of her thrown out on the street,'

said Sarah in a troubled voice. 'I'd feel bad.'

'What sort of household is it?' asked Mrs Miller.

'Just one old lady.'

'There you are,' said Mrs Miller. 'You might feel bad if the girl lost her job, but you would feel worse if you heard that poor old lady was murdered in her bed by the parlour maid and her fancy man!'

'I suppose you're right,' said Sarah wearily. I'll talk to Alfie about it tonight, she thought.

'You just slip upstairs and put that salve on the bruise. It will make it feel a bit better. And after that,' Mrs Miller added, 'you can take that small basket over there and go down to Covent Garden market and buy me a couple of fresh cabbages. A nice walk in the air will do you good. I'll finish the pots.'

'Thank you, Mrs Miller.' Sarah almost felt like weeping – it was so rare that people were kind to her. 'I'm very grateful to you.'

'Well, you can show it by telling me where that girl worked,' said Mrs Miller. 'I think it is my duty to do something about that, Sarah.'

Sarah stared at her. Mrs Miller was very kind, but she was also very stubborn. She would not rest until she had wormed the address out of her. Sarah's mind scuttled around trying to think of an address which would not lead Mrs Miller to Mavis, but her mind was blank: all she could think of was the true address. And then she remembered the empty house, part of the same neat terrace, next door to Mrs Leamington's house.

'It was Number Five, Goodwin's Court,' she said.

Mrs Miller stared at her. 'But I know that place!' she said. 'I knew the woman who cooked there! Just a husband and wife lived there – the pair of them went off to Italy for the year. Very nice people they were too – very rich. Lovely house, my friend told me – full of all sorts of valuables. That Mavis of yours has made a fool out of you. She told you a wrong address. I bet she works in the other side of town. Mark my words, you'll find her down in Pimlico or somewhere like that.'

'The police might be able to track her down,' said Sarah, restraining a smile. 'Thanks for the salve, Mrs Miller, and thanks very much for doing my work. I'll be as quick as I can at the market.'

Mrs Miller was not in the kitchen when Sarah came back downstairs – Sarah hoped that she wasn't in the parlour telling the lady of the house the story about Mavis. Sarah grabbed the basket and went out by the back door as quickly as possible, hoping to avoid any more questions. The fog was not so bad today so she went quickly up the alleyway and turned into Bloomsbury Square.

Suddenly, a tall young man with a huge moustache crossed the road, took Sarah firmly by the arm and walked alongside her, holding her in a grip of steel. The man may have had the same name, but up close, he could not have been more different to Arthur Leamington. The deep tone of his voice, the lean shape of his body, even the cat-like way he moved. This was definitely no toff.

'Make sure that you never say one word about what happened last night,' he hissed menacingly in her ear. 'Friends of mine want me to give you one warning. Are you listening to me? Not a single word.' He shook her slightly. 'Do you understand?'

Sarah could hardly speak for fear, but nodded. 'I understand,' she said, as steadily as she could manage.

'That's good,' he said. 'That's very good. Because if you do talk to anyone, then I will strangle you. Strangling is easy, you know. Your neck wouldn't be the first that I have squeezed the life out of.'

CHAPTER 21

HUNTED

Alfie took two seconds to think. Every exit was blocked except one.

He put the skull back into his shirt and, before Grimston had crossed the floor, Alfie began to climb the chimney for the second time that morning.

Alfie now understood why master chimney sweeps lit fires under their chimney sweeping boys.

Fear has a great effect.

Alfie climbed that chimney as if it was a nut tree in a park. Legs, arms, knees, elbows, hands, feet, all worked as smoothly as a machine, each one of them propelling him up. The soot was not bothering him so much now – perhaps he was used to it, or fear of what Grimston would do to him had banished everything else. Suddenly he was in the main chimney. He would not go left or right, but just straight up – straight up to the roof. There had been a look on the man's face that spelt murder.

Alfie kept his head tilted upwards as he climbed, desperately looking for a hint of light coming from the sky. It's not a big house, he was thinking. Only three storeys high. There won't be any more chimney flues, he thought. The servants must sleep in the attics and no one would have bothered putting in fireplaces for them.

Still, thought Alfie, I must be about three-quarters of the way up now. Soon I might even see a bit of light above me. He climbed steadily. The idea of arriving at the top and being out under the sky was a great spur to him.

And then he thought of Grimston.

What would the man be doing? Not waiting patiently in the kitchen; that was sure.

A picture flashed into his mind of Mutsy, the great rat hunter. When Mutsy knew that a rat was in a wall, he became as patient as any cat. He would lie there for hours if necessary, waiting and watching, and the second the rat made its appearance he would seize it by the neck.

That's what Grimston would do. Wait for him on the roof until he came out of the chimney.

At last, it began to grow lighter. Soon he would be out. Alfie told himself he could be a match for Grimston – ducking around chimneys, slithering down sloping roofs. The way that he was feeling now, he just didn't care.

The chimney pot was a tight squeeze, but eventually he popped out.

He crouched for a moment, taking in a few deep breaths and looking all around him. There seemed to be no sign of Grimston. As fast as he could safely move, he made his way across the rooftop. He knew where he was going. Only a few days ago he had stood at the corner of St Martin's Lane and watched Joe come along the same route. If only he had kept hold of him then, had forced him to tell what he had seen, had not allowed him to go back to that house again, if only he had done *something* . . .

But it was no good thinking about that now – wondering what it was that Joe had actually seen, wondering why the sweeping boy had ended up on the slab in Bow Street police station. His task now was to bring those human bones to Inspector Denham.

Alfie slithered quickly down the roof and peered over the edge. There was no one on the pavement except a blind man sitting hopelessly against the wall, a begging bowl beside him. Alfie took hold of the iron pipe leading from the gutter and slid down to the pavement. With a quick look around he bolted into St Martin's Lane and turned down into New Row.

Soon be in Covent Garden, he told himself. He had to wait for a moment to cross Bedfordbury as a huge lumbering bus drawn by six horses made its way across. He glanced behind him several times while he was waiting, but there was no sign of the heavy figure of Master Grimston.

The bus moved on and Alfie darted across. Suddenly a cart came flying up the road. Wheels rumbling, cart swaying, Grimston was standing up, brutally flogging his poor horse. With only a second to spare, Alfie made the pavement and began running wildly.

Another crossing, but this time there was nothing in the way and Alfie shot across. Now only King Street to go and he would be in the piazza in front of Covent Garden. He would be safe there. The fog had disappeared and the streets were crowded. The piazza would be full of people strolling around; Grimston and his cart would not be able to go at more than walking speed.

Grimston kept close behind Alfie. He was ruthless, slashing with his whip to left and right, and people scattered in front of him. Alfie kept running, though he had a stitch in his side. He was tempted to dodge down an alleyway, but that would be a waste of time and he was desperate to get to Inspector Denham.

He looked back over his shoulder. Grimston was fiddling with a rope – he seemed to be tying it. Alfie saw Tom standing beside a vegetable stall, looking at him open-mouthed.

The next thing Alfie knew he was caught in a choking noose. Grimston had snared him with his rope! By some miracle he managed to stay on his feet, but he could not move without being choked. Alfie stopped dead as the cart came nearer.

Then, a large turnip came flying through the air. It caught Grimston just on the side of his head. He dropped the rope and roared his fury, clutching his cheek. Alfie grinned. Tom always had a deadly aim!

Alfie slipped the rope from his neck, coiled it over his shoulder and ran. There was no chance of Grimston catching him now. He had managed to get the wheel of his cart entangled with a heavy wagon loaded with turnips. That will keep him there for a while, thought Alfie, listening to the angry shouts as he ran, weaving his way in and out of the stalls. By the time he reached Bow Street police station he was soaked in sweat and almost fainting from exhaustion. He barely managed to push the door open and stumble inside.

PC Fairley, PC 24 and PC 29 were in the outer office but Inspector Denham's office was open and empty. Alfie was taken aback for a moment, but he could not afford to wait. He delved into his shirt and pulled out the skull and two leg bones.

'Skeleton of a missing boy, apprentice to Master Grimston,' he gasped. 'Found concealed in a chimney. Name of Isaac.'

CHAPTER 22

GRIMSTON

Instantly PC Fairley sprang into action.

'Grimston,' he growled. 'Well, this will give us a reason to arrest that fellow. You, boy, where can I find him?'

Alfie was so surprised that he could not answer for a minute. Was this the same Constable Fairley who had tried to convict him of Joe's murder by writing down an unfair confession? And now he was all ready to arrest someone else just because of what Alfie had said. Alfie gaped like a fish, but then gulped and said hastily, 'These must be Isaac's bones. He was chasing me. He knew I was bringing the bones to the police. Isaac was one of his boys – he disappeared.'

'We'll get him for murder – for two murders. He probably murdered the boy that you found as well,' said PC Fairley eagerly. 'Leave the bones there,' he said to Alfie. 'Let's go! PC 24 you stay here and tell Inspector Denham what's happening. PC 29, you come with me and we'll arrest this man.' A moment later they were out in the road running through the market.

'There he is!' shouted Alfie, pointing to the cart. The turnip dealer, a heavily-built country man, had grabbed Grimston by the coat and was shaking him like a rat. Alfie waited for a moment, enjoying the shrill sound of the two police whistles blowing. Two more constables joined them, running out from the Covent Garden marketplace. Alfie was tempted to join them but resisted. He drew back. He would keep out of Grimston's way, he decided. His excitement was beginning to die down and doubts were coming into his mind. He looked around. No point in going home. No one would be there. Tom had disappeared, but it wasn't Tom that he wanted to talk to. He needed a cool, keen brain to help him to disentangle all the twists and turns of this mystery.

* * *

The last of the pious ladies who attended morning service at St Martin-in-the-Fields were just disappearing when Alfie joined Sammy on the steps of the church. There was a satisfactory amount of coins on the cap beside him, but for once Alfie did not bother to count them. He was hungry – it seemed a long time since that cake the night before – but he was used to being hungry and at the moment he had more important things on his mind than food.

'Where's Mutsy?' he asked.

'Tom took him a few minutes ago,' said Sammy. 'He said that there was a Punch and Judy show on the steps of St Paul's at Covent Garden. He thought he could get a few pence if he and Mutsy did some tricks when the audience moved away from the puppets. Told me that Grimston was chasing you. Told me about the turnip, too.' Sammy chuckled at the thought.

'Let's go into the church,' said Alfie. He tumbled the coins into his pocket, clapped the cap back onto Sammy's head, grabbed his brother's arm and guided him up the steps and into the church.

It was quite dark inside – dark, and warm from the glowing, coal-filled heater beside the altar and from the people who had prayed there for the last hour. An elderly sacristan was quenching the candles with a small metal hood and he looked around enquiringly when the two boys came in.

'Out you go,' he said sternly, once he had seen them properly.

Alfie hesitated. He must look a terrible sight – his clothes were filthy, stained with soot, and no doubt his face was the same. He was about to retreat, but then found his courage. This church was an ideal place for a chat with Sammy – warm and quiet and, above all, he was safe from Grimston here. There was always the possibility that the man might have been released by the police by now. And if he were, the first thing he would do would be to come looking for Alfie.

Alfie snatched off his cap, and took off Sammy's also. 'Is it all right if me and my brother come in to say a prayer, like?' he asked respectfully.

The sacristan frowned, surveying Alfie from head to toe, but then smiled as he looked at Sammy. 'Our little songbird,' he said. 'Come in, little bird, come into God's house.'

Sammy nudged Alfie, but respectfully answered, 'Thank you, sir.'

Alfie steered him into a seat, glad that the church

was so dark, so the sacristan couldn't see the grin that kept trying to twist his mouth. Little bird, indeed! He would have fun teasing Sammy about that sometime – but not now. Now things were very serious.

The boys sat in silence, faces turned towards the altar until the sacristan left the church. Then Alfie turned his mouth close to Sammy's ear, urgently whispering the story of the morning, the climb up the chimney, finding the skeleton, the arrival of Grimston in the old lady's kitchen, the chase through the London streets and finally the constables' pursuit of Grimston.

Sammy nodded from time to time, but at the end he said, 'It don't make sense.'

'Why not?' Alfie felt annoyed. He had doubts himself, but he had hoped that Sammy would assure him that the case was now solved, that Grimston would be put in prison and that Alfie would be free from his fear that the master chimney sweep would hunt him down and murder him. 'Why don't it make sense?' he asked aggressively.

'None of it makes sense.' Sammy sounded irritated. 'Use your loaf, Alfie! How could Grimston murder a boy and stuff him up a chimney? You was going on about how hard it was for you to get up there. I bet

141

Grimston would make three or four of you. You said he was a big brute of a fellow. He couldn't get up a chimney to save his life, I'd reckon.'

'That's true,' said Alfie. 'I was sort of thinking that myself, but then I thought Grimston might have strangled him, carried him onto the roof and stuffed the body down the . . .' His voice trailed away. Even to himself, this did not sound likely.

'More likely this chimney sweeping boy, Isaac . . . more likely he died in the chimney. Died of breathing in the smoke and the soot. You yourself was telling Tom all about the number of boys that die in chimneys.'

'True enough,' said Alfie, feeling discouraged.

'Must have been there for about a year – likely the rooks ate the flesh from him,' said Sammy thoughtfully. 'But it don't make sense. Why didn't nobody guess? A body stuffed into a chimney! The smoke would have gone pouring back down into the rooms again. No fire could burn at all if a chimney had a boy wedged into it – don't care what you say, Alfie, it just don't make sense to me.'

'No, it don't.' Alfie sat very quietly, looking ahead at the small red light that burned near the altar. He heard his brother chuckle quietly beside him.

'Think!' urged Sammy. 'Remember what the cook told Sarah about the empty house. Remember this afternoon when you went to Bow Street police station. You got a surprise, didn't you?'

Alfie stared at his brother. Sammy had a smile on his face, the corners of his mouth twitching with amusement, his blind eyes staring impassively ahead – looking into his own mind.

'When you told me about the chimney that hadn't been cleaned, I started to work out what had happened,' said Sammy.

Suddenly Alfie understood everything. 'They'd have had to call for the sweep every day,' he said slowly, fitting the pieces of the puzzle together, just to make sure that everything made sense. 'No one could have lit a fire below a blocked chimney like that.'

'So what's the solution?' Sammy turned his face towards his brother. In the dim light Alfie could see his teeth gleam in an amused grin.

Alfie jumped to his feet, burning with excitement. 'Come on, Sam,' he said. 'You and me are going for a little walk.'

CHAPTER 23

WHO IS GUILTY?

A few rays of watery sunlight had come through the clouds by the time that Alfie and Sammy reached Goodwin's Court. They shone down the narrow alley, lighting up the rose-coloured brick paving, the shining, many-paned windows, the rich glow of the brass knockers and the glossy sheen of well-painted doors. There was no one about. Alfie stood at the entrance, but did not go down. He clicked his tongue with annoyance. Goodwin's Court was far too narrow for anyone to see the chimneys.

'Let's go to the other side of St Martin's Lane, Sam,' he said.

Once safely across the road and standing on the pavement, Alfie tilted his head back and surveyed the roofs of the little row of houses. His eyesight was keen and he could plainly see the chimneys. He went along the line of them, counting aloud and then nodded.

He had found out what he had come to see. 'Five chimney stacks for ten houses,' he murmured, annoyed with himself that he hadn't guessed sooner.

'You get it?' enquired Sammy. 'I guessed as soon as you told me about the four different passageways leading from the main chimney, and that no one had found the skeleton sooner.'

'I get it,' replied Alfie, and he punched Sammy on the arm to show that he had no hard feelings about Sammy working it out first.

'Let's go down and see how the ladies of Number Four are faring after their exciting morning,' he said with a chuckle.

'I won't come in, haven't had time to have a wash – been too busy with the police. Just wanted to ask how you all were, after the shock, you know?' said Alfie, all in one breath, as soon as Ellen opened the door.

'Is that Alfie? Come on in.' Mrs Bailey appeared.

'Come and have something to eat, the two of you, and tell us what's been happening. The missus is out. Gone to see her daughter. Never mind the dirt. That floor is marble – it wipes up easily. Come into the kitchen. We have a great fire going there. You can warm yourselves by it. And not a trace of smoke. Lucky we don't need that Mr Grimston back again in a hurry – he went off in a great rush after you left, said he was feeling very ill. Even the mistress didn't believe him. "Stands to reason that man knows something about the skeleton," she said. "I never did trust him," that's what I said to her and that's the truth, isn't it, Ellen?'

The kitchen fire was burning brightly. Certainly there was no trace of smoke around, but that was not surprising. Poor little Isaac's body had been mainly in the unused chimney passage, but a foot had been in the main chimney. Perhaps he had dived down the unused chimney to get away from the smoke and heat when a fire had been lit below in order to make him get out quickly. The soot had piled up around the body and that and the foot had prevented the smoke from escaping freely. Alfie was quietly confident that the solution was correct. Still, he needed a little more information before he could set a trap.

'Where's the other lady? The parlour maid?' he asked, looking around.

'Lady!' snorted the cook. 'Fine lady that one! She's taken herself off. Good riddance to bad rubbish! Didn't sleep in her bed last night. I've had my suspicions of her for many a long month. Kept bad company, Mavis, she did – her and her fancy man.'

'You don't tell me!' marvelled Alfie. 'Responsible job and all that. I suppose she had the keys to everything. Someone was telling me that she even had the keys to the empty house next door.'

'Well, I don't know who's been telling you she had keys to next door,' said the cook. 'That she certainly did not! I know where the rumour might have started, though. When the couple next door first started talking about going off to Italy for a year, they wanted Mrs Leamington to have the keys, really pressed her. But my mistress said no. "You've got all those valuable paintings in there – I wouldn't sleep at night worrying about them – ask the police to keep an eye on the place." That's what she said. Mr Arthur, her son, well, he thought she was being very disobliging to old friends, but she wouldn't budge. Ever so upset he was! Lost his temper with his poor old mother. I think that he had a mind to do it himself. I heard him knock on their door, anyway, just afterwards.'

'Tell us what the police said when you brought them bones along,' said Ellen eagerly. 'I nearly had a heart attack when you came out of the chimney with that skull!'

'Give the lad a chance, Ellen,' said the cook, but her own eyes were bright with curiosity. 'Here, have a piece of my fruit cake, and one for your brother. Here you are, Sammy, it's just there, just by your hand. So, Alfie, when you got to the police station . . . ?'

On the way back towards Covent Garden, nicely warmed through with hot milk and fruit cake, Alfie speculated about about what he had heard. Since she never had the keys, Mavis and her cracksman had nothing to do with it. Arthur Leamington, though . . . Alfie could just picture the scene. The polite knock on the door next door. What would he have said? 'Apologise for my mother – getting very old – worries, you know – happy to oblige – no trouble.' And how had the couple in Number Five replied?

Perhaps they said yes. Perhaps Arthur Leamington had the keys to the house and was able to go in and out as he pleased. And perhaps come out the back door to the mews with a parcel carefully wrapped in brown paper under his arm, and climb into his gig . . .

But then one day he was seen by a chimney sweep . . .

Alfie's mind darted through the possibilities. Only one of them really made sense to him. But first of all he had to get evidence.

'Sam,' he said in a low voice. 'I have a plan and I need your help.'

The great thing about Sammy, he thought, as he explained his plan, was that he had such a quick mind. He never needed lengthy explanations. Now he listened carefully, nodded his head from time to time, and made a few useful suggestions of his own.

The plan was made. The trap would be sprung before another hour was over.

Tom was still outside St Paul's, the church on the piazza at Covent Garden. The crowd was dispersing and the Punch and Judy show puppets were being packed away in boxes ready for the next day's performances.

'Tom, would you take Sammy down to Bow Street police station? He has a message to deliver from me to Inspector Denham.' Alfie stroked Mutsy. He wished that he could take the big dog with him, but no dog could go where he was going this afternoon. 'Oh, and thanks for that turnip, Tom,' he added. 'You saved me! I bet old Grimston had a sore face after that.'

'He's in there with the police at the station, you know,' said Tom, chuckling. 'I saw the horse and cart tied up in that yard of theirs, just next to the police gig. They must be still asking him questions. I suppose he was the one that murdered Joe.'

'Nice collection.' Alfie was looking down at Tom's cap. It would take too long to bring Tom up to date, he decided. He was on fire to get on with his plan. 'You could get some sausages with that after Sammy has given his message,' he said. 'Wait for me, though, before you put them on the pan. I'll be back in about a couple of hours.' I hope, he added silently.

Pity about that fire that they had lit in the kitchen – and probably in the other rooms, also – of Number Four, he thought as he walked back towards St Martin's Lane. How hot would they make the chimney, he wondered? Still he would just have to manage. Luckily the few gleams of sun had gone and the fog was starting to come back again. Normally Alfie hated fog, but today he thought he would really welcome a good old 'London Particular', a real peasouper where the people on foot groped around as if they were blind, and a man took his life in his hands when he crossed the road.

The fog was beginning to come down quite thickly by the time that Alfie climbed the handy downpipe on St Martin's Lane. The roofs were wet and slippery, but he edged his way carefully across. He could not afford to slip and break his neck now. As he went, he repeated to himself Joe's last words – broken phrases that would stay with him for the rest of his life: a bend . . . something about going the wrong way or into the wrong room . . . something about being scared . . . Poor Joe!

Justice for Joe – wasn't that what Inspector Denham had said? Perhaps today was going to be the day when Joe got justice.

When he reached the chimney, he heard the bell from St Martin's Church ring out the hour. Four o'clock. Not enough time for Sammy to have done his errand, he told himself. Half past four would be more like it. He squatted down beside the smoky warmth and prepared to wait.

And then, he thought, he would find out for certain what Joe's last words meant.

And who had killed the poor little chimney sweep.

CHAPTER 24

SAMMY DELIVERS
A MESSAGE

Bow Street police station was noisy when Tom, leaving Mutsy outside, escorted Sammy into its coal-smelling interior. PC Fairley was writing at a desk, PC 22 was looking through some papers, PC 31 was making tea, pouring the water from a blackened kettle into an almost as black teapot, and PC 35 was polishing his boots.

From one of the cells came the sound of someone kicking the wall and then of an angry voice shouting, 'Let me out of here! You've no right to keep me here. I know nothing about any boys. It's nothing to do with me if some bones turn up in a chimney. Birds bring things and drop them down. Everyone knows that. Let me out!'

Tom grinned. He recognised Grimston's voice, and Sammy had just told him the story of the bones in the chimney. It was nice to hear a bully getting his come-uppance.

'Could I speak to Inspector Denham, please?' Sammy turned his face from one side of the room to the other, calmly waiting to face the answerer.

There was a moment's silence. Sammy waited. The men would be looking uncomfortably at one another, he guessed. People were always embarrassed when a blind person addressed them. Never bothered him, but it bothered them.

And then the inner door opened. 'Is that Alfie's brother? Come in, Sammy. And Tom, isn't it? I remember you.'

'We can't come in, sir.' Tom had been well rehearsed by Alfie. *Don't go into the inner office*, his cousin had said. *Make sure that you stay in the outer office.* 'We've got our dog waiting outside,' he continued, 'and he's all wet and muddy.'

'We just brought you a message from Alfie,' said Sammy calmly and clearly. 'He wants to see you. He wanted to know if he could see you in about an hour's time – if you won't mind waiting until then, sir. First of all he has to check out something back at Goodwin's Court. He thinks he's found some evidence to show who murdered Joe.'

'I hope he's not getting himself into trouble.' The inspector frowned and Tom thought he looked angry, but Sammy heard the anxiety in the man's voice. The inspector seemed to care about poor people like himself and his brother – and about a chimney sweep boy called Joe.

'Oh no, sir,' said Sammy. 'Alfie is clever. He didn't have time to tell us exactly what he had found or what it means. Just to say he'd be over to see you shortly.'

Someone had been stirring water vigorously, but at those words they stopped and the scratch of a quill pen ceased. Sammy fumbled for Tom's arm and gripped it tightly, turning his cousin towards the doorway. He had one more sentence to deliver but he would wait until Tom had opened the door. When the rush of the damp, cold air hit his face, he turned back and spoke again, loud and clear.

'Alfie said to remind you about what you said. He said to tell you that today will be the day when you can get justice for Joe.'

And then, Tom, half choking with giggles, steered Sammy towards the market.

Their work was not yet done. Wait for ten minutes before you go back in again, Alfie had ordered.

CHAPTER 25

THE TRAP IS SPRUNG

Alfie crouched on the rooftop and felt uncomfortable. He didn't even admit it to himself, but he hated being so high up. It wasn't that he was afraid of heights – he had often scaled a high wall to get away from an angry stallholder. No, it was more that it felt sort of lonely up there – nobody around, no voices, no people passing, no funny things like a toff slipping in the mud to laugh about, no backchat with the road sweepers, no smells of food cooking – even the noise of the carts and carriages on the roads seemed muted. Only the high, lonely cries of seagulls overhead to listen to and the faint warmth of the chimney stack to cling to.

From his place beside the chimney, Alfie could not see down into the court. That was a nuisance. However, he had set the trap, laid the bait and he just had to hope that it would work. Goodwin's Court was a quiet place and every sound made down there floated up to him. He heard a door bang, light, hurried footsteps going across the brick-paved surface – a scullery maid going out to a shop for something, he thought. He heard a window open and then shut again.

But then he turned his eyes towards the mews at the back of the houses, and heard what he was waiting for. The fog was too thick to see much but there was the whinny of a horse, the noise of wheels – a cart or a gig, only Sammy would be sure about which it was – and then the click of the gate leading from the mews into the yard.

At that moment the bell from St Martin's church chimed the half-hour.

Alfie did not hesitate. Like a shadow in the fog, he slipped over into the chimney, clinging on to its edge until his feet found a slight unevenness in its brick lining – somewhere that his bare toes could cling to until he got the rest of his body inside the chimney. Then slowly and cautiously, one hand at a time, he let go of the parapet.

Alfie wriggled his way, careful not to go too fast. The light grew fainter as he went down and he did not want to risk missing the side passages of the first floor.

His feet felt warm, and then the warmth rushed up past his face, smoke – hot smoke! For a moment he almost panicked, picturing the glowing fire in the kitchen of Number Four. By now they would have lit a fire in the dining room too; the old lady would have returned to find a fire in the drawing room where she would sit until her evening meal was ready. Fires everywhere and burning, stinging smoke rushing up the chimney.

Alfie was choking, drowning in smoke. And then his sliding foot felt another opening. The first floor passages. Just in time, he thought, still trying to hold his breath. He turned sharply to the right, hoping that in the smoke-filled darkness he had not become disorientated.

Alfie fumbled in the blackness, bending down to the level of his knees. There were piles of soot here and the walls were heavily coated with it. This was the place where he had found the bones of the boy

Isaac. This was where Joe had gone wrong – perhaps he had found the bones and decided to go down the passageway next to it. Possibly he had not made a mistake, but was looking for a place to dump the bones, to get them out of the way, to stop them blocking the chimney at Number Four. Joe would have feared Grimston's anger if he had arrived down into Number Four with the bones.

Alfie made a quick decision. The smoke was making him choke. He inserted his head into the unswept passageway, sticking his arms out ahead of him and twisting his shoulders. To his relief, he fitted well. This was easier. The passageway sloped downwards, so he could move himself along by scrabbling with his hands and edging forward inch by inch.

There was no smoke here! The chimney was stone cold – it hadn't been used for almost a year!

Now Alfie knew that he was right. That his gamble had paid off.

The end of the sloping passage came quite quickly. He felt the edge of it with his fingers. There was no room to stand up. Still keeping his hands in front of his head, Alfie dived into the downward passage.

As he had expected, he went quickly at first. Once

he felt himself stick, then he went back to his old routine, wriggling and twisting, edging himself, inch by inch. There was no smoke in his face and he felt none of the panic that had gripped him earlier that day. Now it was just an unpleasant job, rather like skinning eels, something that had to be got through in order to bring a result.

There was a faint light ahead of him now. Soon he would come out and what would he see then?

The fireplace was wide and the last few yards were easy. As soon as his hands met the hearthstone, Alfie twisted his shoulders and wriggled out.

Beside him was something round and spiky – a chimney sweep's brush. On the white rug in front of the fireplace were two small sooty footprints.

Poor Joe! He must have left his brush behind in his haste to flee the room when he first discovered it. When he'd gone back for the brush, he'd been seized and strangled. Perhaps put in a sack, taken out by the kitchen door into the yard behind. A yard which led to the mews where someone had left his gig.

Alfie got to his feet and looked around. He was in a large, beautifully decorated room, well lit by the street gas lamp outside the window.

Sammy and he had guessed correctly. The chimney

had been built to serve both Number Four and Number Five. It made sense. The houses had been built as a terrace – ten houses, but there were only five chimney stacks, each main chimney shaft serving two houses.

He had come down into Number Five, the empty house next door to Number Four, the house where the owners had gone off to Italy, leaving all their valuables.

This was obviously a drawing room. The furniture was all draped with white linen dustsheets, and, beneath the cloths, Alfie could see the shapes of armchairs and sofas, small tables and tall cupboards.

The walls were covered with green striped wallpaper, made to look like silk. Alfie noticed something strange about them – there were ghostly oblongs of lighter paper, about six on each of the three walls facing him. Pictures must have hung there, year after year, protecting the wallpaper while the dust and smoke had darkened the rest of it.

In one of the oblongs was a metal door. Alfie, curious as always, crossed over to it. The door had been pushed closed, but when Alfie inserted a sooty finger, it swung open.

A safe, thought Alfie. The butcher that he sometimes worked for had one of these. He put all his coins into it every day, piling them into little linen bags and taking the bags to the bank at the end of every week.

But this safe was completely empty. Some safe-breaker had opened it and emptied it while the owners were in Italy. For a moment, Alfie thought of Mavis and her cracksman boyfriend. Maybe Tom was right, and she was mixed up in Joe's murder after all . . .

But a professional cracksman would have made a neater job of it, Alfie realised. This safe bore the marks of a hammer and chisel. The lock had been smashed by brute force.

Suddenly Alfie heard footsteps coming up the stairs. He quickly looked for a hiding place, but then decided to stay where he was. He had to be sure that he was right.

The door opened and the man stood there, his tall stovepipe hat in his hand. He wore a pair of strong boots, a waterproof cape, a blue jacket with a turned-up collar. And in that collar, a badge. PC 27.

It was PC Fairley himself.

CHAPTER 26

MURDERER

'Murderer!' screamed Alfie, and at the same moment PC Fairley hurled his steel-hardened top hat across the floor. It missed Alfie's legs by an inch.

By this time Alfie had already inserted his head and body back into the chimney. Once he got to the main chimney, he wedged his body into the neighbouring passage.

And then he waited. He did not have long to wait!

A shot from a revolver came up the chimney, the bullet dislodging clouds of soot. Alfie buried his head in his arms and grinned to himself. He was safe here. He was out of the way of any shots and PC Fairley would not be able to climb the chimney.

And then there was a roar from the drawing room. 'Put that gun down! By Jupiter, I'll see you hanged for this.'

Alfie wriggled forward and managed to get his hands, knees and then feet into the main shaft then back into the drawing room flue. He wanted to witness this.

Another roar, even louder this time. 'Face that wall! Put your hands up! Constable, search him and then handcuff him.'

At these words, Alfie wriggled his way back down into the room.

'So there you are, popping out like a jack-in-the-box!' Inspector Denham's face was red with fury, but a reluctant grin spread over it at the sight of Alfie.

'Where are Sammy and Tom?' asked Alfie.

'I sent them home,' said the inspector. 'No place for a blind boy with a dangerous criminal and child murderer around.' He glared at PC Fairley who stared impassively ahead. His hands were fastened together behind his back by a pair of iron handcuffs and he had a bruise on one cheekbone.

'You can't prove anything,' he snarled. 'I came here because of a message that this house was being burgled. Unfortunately I arrived too late.' His eyes swept the walls where the marks of the stolen pictures were clearly visible on the silky wallpaper.

'Nothing stolen today – so far,' said Alfie smartly. He went up to one of the oblongs and blew hard. A cloud of dust rose from it. 'That picture has been gone for weeks. I reckon, sir,' Alfie went on, addressing the inspector, 'that Constable Fairley has been nice and quietly removing these pictures ever since the owners gave him the house keys at the police station for safekeeping, rather than leave them with Arthur Leamington. The constable took them one by one. Much easier to get rid of them that way – Mary the Fence at St Giles told me that.' Alfie noticed that PC Fairley gave a start at that name, but he pretended not to notice and carried on. '"Two or three pictures might cause questions,"' he said, trying to make his voice husky like Mary the Fence's. '"One at a time is the way to get rid of them".' He reverted to his own voice and addressed PC Fairley. 'And you've been working on it ever since the owners went on holiday, ain't you? And then, of course, you had another bit of luck because one of them pictures was hiding a safe. Nasty job you made of it, too!' Alfie eyed the damaged safe with an air of scorn.

'You . . .' PC Fairley hurled himself at Alfie, who neatly sidestepped, allowing the man to crash to the ground.

'He was probably banging away at that when poor old Joe came out of the chimney.' Alfie looked at the prostrate body of the evil policeman with satisfaction. 'Joe heard the tapping and came down – or else perhaps he was going to leave the bones of poor little Isaac in this empty house, we'll never know. Anyway, he went back up smartish when he saw a policeman. He was so scared that he went right up to the top and when he saw me below in St Martin's Lane he came down to talk to me.' Alfie stopped there. If only Joe had not been so scared, if only he had told Alfie exactly what he had seen. Still, it was no good thinking like that, so he swallowed hard and continued. 'Joe came down to talk to me, but he was too frightened to tell me the whole story. And he was so scared of Grimston that he went back to finish off cleaning the chimney of Number Four, and had to come back here to get the brush he'd forgotten. Nothing much else for him to do, poor little fellow. And of course PC Fairley was waiting for him. He strangled him and shoved the body into his gig. Meant to throw it in the river, but his aim weren't too good.'

'It's all a pack of lies.' PC Fairley had struggled to his feet. 'You killed him yourself.'

'Inspector Denham is going to get a shock when he finds the amount of money you have stacked up in your house or in your bank,' said Alfie with a grin. 'And that tidy little gig you have. Not too many constables can afford a gig, can they? And, of course,' he said with a sudden flash of inspiration, 'Mary the Fence will give evidence against you. Good friend of mine, Mary the Fence. Told me the whole story. She'd bear witness against her own grandchildren if she thought it would save her skin.'

'If she says a word about me, I'll see she goes to jail too, even if I have to swing for it,' growled PC Fairley.

Alfie smiled to himself. It was good to find one of his guesses was right. He had no pity to spare for a man who had strangled an unfortunate little fellow like Joe.

'I think I have heard enough,' said Inspector Denham grimly. 'Constable, take the suspect downstairs. I'll follow you in a minute.'

'What will happen to Grimston, inspector?' asked Alfie when the constable and his prisoner had gone heavily down the stairs.

The inspector gave an impatient sigh. 'I suppose I'll have to release him,' he said, his voice sounding annoyed. 'If he didn't have anything to do with Joe's death, then I've nothing to hold him on.'

'Isaac?' queried Alfie.

'I know what the inquest will say about that,' grunted the inspector. '"Death by misadventure." That's what they'll say. "The lad was careless." I sometimes wonder whether those magistrates have a scrap of humanity in them.'

He stumped down the stairs and Alfie followed, leaving sooty footsteps on the red carpet. Couldn't be helped, he thought, looking at the marks. What did he care if he messed up their carpet? The owners would get some scullery maid or someone who was paid about ten pounds a year to clean the place up before they came back into it. They'd be furious, anyway, when they found that they had lost their pictures and perhaps some other valuables from out of the safe. But there was something else on Alfie's mind so he didn't waste time thinking about the owners of Number Five.

'Sir,' he said.

'Yes, Alfie?' The inspector had the bunch of keys that the constable had taken from PC Fairley's pocket. He held them up. 'I didn't know that he had the keys to this place. It must have been arranged before he came to Bow Street police station.' Inspector Denham seemed to feel the need to explain himself, but Alfie had something else on his mind.

'Sir,' he said, 'before you let out Grimston, is there anything that can be done for those three boys he keeps in a stable in Devil's Acre? He'll be in such a mood that he might take it out on them. The little fellow, Bert, looks real sick. I'd say he'll be the next body in the chimney.'

The inspector nodded. 'I'll keep Grimston in for another day. I can easily hold him a bit longer for questioning. I'll have a word with a friend of mine; he's the master of Marylebone workhouse – a decent place. I'm sure he'll oblige me and take the three boys in for a couple of years and teach them a skill – shoe-making or something like that.'

'That's good,' said Alfie. His own father had made a reasonable living between making new shoes and repairing old ones, before he died of blood poisoning.

'I'll keep an eye on Grimston. There is a law against using boys as young as that to climb chimneys. The trouble is that the magistrates just warn them not to do it again and nothing happens.' The inspector's voice was subdued.

'He probably didn't murder Isaac,' said Alfie soothingly. 'I'd say that it wasn't murder. I'd say that he died from the smoke or the soot. It's not a nice job, sir. Myself, I've made up my mind that this is the last time that I'll ever go up a chimney.'

Alfie was conscious of a flat feeling. He had solved the murder, but there was no feeling of jubilation, no excitement, no instinct to go out and celebrate. This was not an occasion for festivity. Two very young boys were dead and there was no getting away from that fact.

Inspector Denham seemed to sense what he was thinking. He locked the door behind them and looked down at Alfie. 'You did what you set out to do,' he said quietly, 'and many a man could not say the same. You got justice for Joe.'

CHAPTER 27

THE FLEA CIRCUS

'Anyone at home?'

Alfie woke with a start. They had all stayed up very late discussing the murder. When Jack came back from taking Sarah home, they had gone on talking, reliving the funny bits – especially about Old Grimston and the rats – and eventually just dropped off to sleep one by one.

'Coming,' he called. Accompanied by Mutsy, he unbolted the door a moment later and blinked.

There on the doorstep was the sergeant from Bow Street police station. He held an envelope in his hand. 'Message from Inspector Denham,' he said.

'Wants me to bust a gang of bank robbers?' enquired Alfie cheerfully. 'Cracksmen, magsmen, snotter-haulers, hoisters, fogle-hunters – Alfie Sykes at his service.'

'Now don't you get cheeky,' reproved the sergeant. 'Inspector Denham sent you these – they're tickets for a show. He was going to bring his own boys but they've all got the measles.' He held out the envelope and then dug in his pocket. 'And here's five shillings for you. Inspector Denham said that you should buy yourself some sweets and that you would find a use for whatever is left over.'

Alfie's eyes sparkled at the sight of the five silver coins. He quickly slid them into his pocket and took the envelope from the policeman's hand. He sent his thanks to the inspector and politely hoped that his family would soon recover.

'What are the tickets for?' asked Tom, coming to join him once the door was closed.

Alfie took the envelope to the light of the small window set high up in the wall of the cellar. 'Some sort of play or something, I suppose,' he said as he drew out four tickets. 'I don't suppose . . .' And then he stopped. His eyes widened as he read. 'A flea circus!' His exclamation woke up Jack and Sammy.

'What! Real fleas?' Jack was puzzled but Sammy had heard some children talking about a circus of fleas.

They were still discussing it when Sarah came in bursting with excitement. She had just got a new job as waitress at the White Horse Inn in Haymarket and had been invited to spend an afternoon getting to know the place before starting work in two weeks' time.

'It's so lucky that it's my afternoon off,' she said, then added, 'What are you all looking so excited about?'

St Martin's church bell was sounding one o'clock by the time that they finished telling her the story of Constable Fairley and, of course, about the tickets to the flea circus. They walked with Sarah as far as the White Horse and then left her to go up towards Leicester Square.

The flea circus did not open until two o'clock but Alfie wanted to take a lot of time to choose sweets. Three of the five shillings had gone into the rent box – it was Alfie's dread that one bad week would come when money for the rent could not be found and then they would all be thrown out on the street – and one of the shillings was reserved for a good supper, but with the last shilling he was determined to buy sweets for the gang. He had never tasted sweets, but had seen rich children sucking them, tossing them into their mouths with expressions of ecstasy and begging parents to buy them. He had often stood in front of the windows of sweet-shops wondering how they tasted.

The sweet-shop in Leicester Square was thronged with children – well-off children in warm coats, knitted stockings and shining leather boots.

'One pennyworth each,' said one parent and others echoed this. Alfie marched up to the counter and casually took the bright silver shilling from his pocket.

'I want a shilling's worth of sweets,' he said loudly and clearly, and saw with satisfaction how these well-dressed children stared at him. They couldn't believe their ears – these four ragged boys were each having three times as many sweets as they were. 'All right if we look around a bit and make up our minds?' he added.

That told them, thought Alfie with satisfaction as he marched down the line of shelves reading the names aloud for Sammy.

Tom, he noticed, had stayed at the counter, unable to wait. He knew how he felt – his own mouth was watering, but he was determined to make a good choice.

'They're Bulls' Eyes,' said the shopkeeper as Tom pointed towards some round white and black sweets. 'Pennyworth? There you are. And the humbugs – another pennyworth. Toffees? Fizz balls?' Rapidly he twisted some paper into a cone shape, tipped in the sweets and handed it to Tom.

The smell coming from the jars and boxes was glorious. Alfie tried to think how to describe the sweets to Sammy. 'The next ones are called bootlaces . . . Peggy legs are long – about the length of your hand and about as thick as two of your fingers'

'Let him try a little bit,' said the shop man, his eye on the shilling in Alfie's hand. Quickly he sliced one of the long, black bootlaces into four and gave a piece to each boy. 'That's liquorice, that is.'

Alfie made a face and looked at Sammy.

'Don't like it,' said Sammy decisively. 'I'll take a peggy leg, that'll last a good long time if it's as big as you say and I'll have two pence worth of Turkish Delight. I like the sound of that name. You get something different, Alfie, and then we can share.'

The poster outside the Alhambra Theatre in Leicester

Square was bigger than a man. Alfie stopped and read the words done in huge letters of red on a yellow background.

WORLD FAMOUS FLEA CIRCUS
Russian fleas – 200 of them
Watch them on roundabouts, swings, tightrope
Acrobat fleas
Turkish fleas – new to this country –
pulling stage-coaches
An omnibus pulled by four fleas
A padlock and chain pulled by just one flea
See Napoleon seated on horseback –
all done by French fleas

An hour passed as quickly as five minutes while Alfie and the others wandered here and there looking at all the wonders. A few people stared at the four ragged boys with surprise, but Alfie didn't care. His money was as good as theirs, he thought.

'You look like you've plenty of fleas,' said a well-dressed young gentleman, staring at Alfie in a challenging way. He was about the same age as Alfie, but was wearing a black silk waistcoat, with a gold watch prominently displayed, and a starched shirt, with the pointed collar standing upright under his chin.

'None today, sorry,' said Alfie briskly. 'All promised to the Russians. Come back next week and I'll see what I can do for you.'

He was pleased to hear the laugh that burst out from the other children. The boy with the black silk waistcoat didn't seem popular with any of them. One girl in particular seemed to find the joke very funny. Alfie winked at Tom, nudged Sammy and went on calmly explaining to his brother about how the flea was towing the carriage by means of a fine gold wire attached to one hind leg.

'Made by a Swiss clockmaker to show off his skill, I understand,' said one well-dressed toff to another, and the other recited at the top of his voice. 'Great fleas have little fleas upon their backs to bite 'em, and little fleas have lesser fleas, and so ad infinitum.'

'Oh, Papa,' said his daughter, the girl who had laughed so uproariously at Alfie's joke. She was nicely dressed in a coat of scarlet wool and a white fur hat. 'Parents are so embarrassing, aren't they?' she said to Alfie, who wasn't quite sure how to respond. He would have thought that having a rich parent like that gentleman smoking the cigar would be a very useful thing. He winked at her and turned back to Sammy.

'Come on, Beatrice,' said the man who had recited the poem about the fleas. 'Time for supper.'

'I hate supper, don't you?' The girl named Beatrice ignored her father and addressed herself to Alfie.

'Depends on what it is,' said Alfie. Stale or mouldy bread wasn't very nice but nothing at all was even worse.

Beatrice made a face. 'We always have something like semolina, or cold rice pudding, or milk and bread, disgusting messes like that.'

'Do you?' Alfie was amazed. It sounded almost as bad as the mouldy bread. 'Me and my mates are going to have a slap-up supper. Some big fat German sausages, some pork pies —'

'What!' interrupted Beatrice, her blue eyes stretched so widely that they looked enormous. She gave a quick look at her father but he was laughing over a joke with his friend. 'Papa would say that we would not be able to sleep if we had a meal like that.'

'Oh, we don't go to sleep afterwards, do we, lads?' Alfie gave a laugh at the thought of that. 'We just sit around a fire and drink hot beer and go to bed when we're sleepy. Get up when we like, too.'

'Beer!' she breathed, gazing at him with admiration and then followed her father. At the door she turned and waved back at Alfie.

'You're so lucky,' she called.

Alfie waved back and then grinned to himself. He thought of all the times when he was cold, hungry and terrified; the times when there was not a crust to eat, no coal for the fire and no money in the rent box.

Still, he thought, we have good times as well as bad. And today was one of the best!

ACKNOWLEDGEMENTS

Thanks are due to my family for their support and help; to my agent, Peter Buckman, for his dedication and encouragement, to the team at Piccadilly Press, especially Melissa Hyder, Vivien Tesseras and Natasha Barnden, and last, but not least, to my editor Anne Clark, a genuinely creative editor with that streak of perfectionism that balances my slap-dash nature. Thanks, Anne, for all your help – sorry about the chimneys.

The London Murder Mysteries

www.piccadillypress.co.uk/londonmurdermysteries

Head online to find out more
about Alfie's world!

The London Murder Mysteries

The MONTGOMERY MURDER

The police must move fast to catch the killer of wealthy Mr Montgomery. They need an insider, some-one streetwise, cunning, bold ... someone like Alfie. When Inspector Denham makes him an offer, Alfie and his gang must sift clues, shadow suspects and negotiate a sinister world of double-dealing and danger.

The DEADLY FIRE

A man's body lies in the burnt-out
wreckage of the Ragged School.
The police say the fire was just an accident –
but Alfie suspects foul play.
Determined to find out the truth, Alfie and his gang
must follow up each clue, investigate every suspect and
risk their lives on the dangerous streets of Victorian
London – until the ruthless murderer is caught.

THE LONDON MURDER MYSTERIES

MURDER ON STAGE

A scream rings out through the theatre. The man on
stage is dead! Who killed him? Alfie has a few suspects
in his sights. But when the spotlight turns on
Alfie himself, the search for the murderer becomes
a fight for his own survival.

THE BODY IN THE FOG

The body lies beneath a statue in Trafalgar Square.
Alfie and his gang set out to find the murderer, just as a
thick fog turns the London streets into a sinister maze.
But soon Alfie is plunged into a still more terrifying
world hidden below the city . . .

Coming soon

SAXBY SMART
PRIVATE DETECTIVE

SIMON CHESHIRE

Be the sleuth yourself and crack all the cases!

In each story Saxby Smart – schoolboy detective – gives you, the reader, clues which help solve the mystery. Are you 'smart' enough to find the answers?

The **Curse** of the **Ancient** **Mask**

A mysterious curse, suspicious sabotage of a school competition, and a very unpleasant relative all conspire to puzzle Saxby Smart, schoolboy private detective.
Stories include: *The Curse of the Ancient Mask*, *The Mark of the Purple Homework* and *The Clasp of Doom*.

The Hangman's Lair

A terrifying visit to the Hangman's Lair to recover stolen money, a serious threat of blackmail, and a mystery surrounding a stranger's unearthly powers test Saxby to the limit in this set of case files!
Stories include: *The Hangman's Lair*, *Diary of Fear* and *Whispers from the Dead*.

www.saxbysmart.co.uk